Just

An anthology of work by the Riverside Writers from Cheddar in Somerset.

Margaret Castle

Jennie Colton

Angela Cornborough

Sally Green

Penny Harden

Jude Painter

Sue Purkiss (Editor)

Heather Redman

Caroline Woolley

Our special thanks go to Huw and Jo and all the staff at the Riverside in Cheddar, who host us each week and look after us so well.

For more information about the Riverside Writers, visit

suepurkisswriter.com

Margaret Castle

Rather than doing a short piece of work each week, as members of the class usually do, Margaret is working on a novel. But she still manages to incorporate whatever it is we've been doing in each session. Very clever! Ed.

Towards the end of our class, Sue suggests homework to expand on what we may have discussed during class, which normally we carry out. This, as you can see from the contents of this book, varies considerably, but is often a short story. Most of us do this with considerable expertise – but not me. I have always written in too many characters, too much story, too much of everything! Sue had the idea I might cope better by writing a long story.

Bingo!

I have now made up a family of characters, who travel through my various homeworks, gradually revealing their progress to me. I can use my overactive imagination. It is an interesting way for me to write. Sometimes I incorporate a poem, relevant to a character, if our homework has been to write a poem; sometimes someone in our group suggests I develop a character in a certain way, which I have a go at, if possible. Below is the first chapter, written in November 2014 and also a recent episode written in April 2017. I may never finish. It's an adventure, the latest episode of which I read out in my turn in class. Everyone in our group has become involved in some way. I value criticism and encouragement, which it turns out is more or less the same! The worst sin is to be boring or incoherent or both, which I constantly endeavour to avoid.

I started by creating a family: Justin Kerr, 40; Danish wife Clara, 38; and twins Zoe and Carl, 6. Justin is a bank manager, based in a small town in Suffolk. The bank closes. Everyone is made redundant except Justin. He is a keen linguist, partly self-taught. He finds himself transferred to Canary Wharf, where his language skills are useful. Clara is a full-time mother, who loves their cottage and rural location and lifestyle. She is very resentful of Justin's attempts to move the family to London. I introduce more people as I proceed. The story continues to develop.

First Chapter

Justin stood four floors up, feeling stranded. Frederico, whom he'd skyped, was in New York for two years and he'd advertised to let this modern flat internally through the bank magazine. Even so the rent was eye-watering; the space hardly more than a generous tool shed. Justin's view through the shifting branches of the plane trees was fractured. The cool autumn wind blew a carrier bag across Soho Square. He was obsessed by his inner vision of geese across the marshes, their calls and then their silences. He yearned for the big open skies of Suffolk. This view gave him a messy roofscape and satellite dishes. Even when he was a child in Wimbledon, home had faced the Common.

He'd been working at Canary Wharf now for two months. It hadn't been all bad. He rolled his shoulders to relieve tension in his lean frame. He still ran each day, very early, in the autumn pre-dawn. It wasn't as satisfying as running along Suffolk's remote country lanes, but he saw foxes on occasion skulking away; sometimes they might pause from scavenging through a bin-bag and stare.

His thoughts ran to the small team he was working with, all urban. He'd overheard someone referring to him as the Country Boy; he'd turned and grinned. After all it was more or less true. He was at least relieved that he wasn't struggling in his new position on the Far East Desk. Though his language skills had brought him here, saved him from redundancy, he wondered if he could adjust sufficiently to really fit in.

Then there was Clara and the twins. He'd cleared with Frederico to allow the family to visit. There was a sofa bed for the children to share. It hadn't gone entirely well. Six year old Zoe and Carl had pillow fought and broken a very classy lamp, which Clara had spent half a day along Oxford Street trying to replace.

Having partly recovered from the setback, the highlight for Justin and the twins was on the Sunday. He'd bought tickets for the family day upstairs at the jazz club round the corner. Jazz was played all day, but there had been the chance to try some of the instruments. The band was great. Both children had joined in and had fun. Clara was cool, distant towards him throughout. Justin tried not to think ahead, for it was difficult to get Clara to talk, really talk, even on his visits home.

Now, walking along Brewer Street, he decided there were some reasons to be cheerful; his Mandarin was improving, Cantonese acceptable. Justin was working alongside Ling. Ling – helpful, outgoing and in his late twenties – had moved from the Hong Kong office. His grandmother had left years earlier with her late husband and lived in China Town where he was living too along with his cousin. Justin, after initially being hesitant about accepting the invitation, was approaching China Town arch, where, somewhere beyond, he'd been invited for supper. The emptiness he felt, nothing to do with hunger, was partly assuaged by the noise, bustle and racket of his surroundings. In this chaos he doubted he'd find the address given him.

He resorted to his phone. The block of flats was fronted by red doors. He pressed the number given him. Cantonese came over the air. After a moment, he gathered himself and announced his name. There was a loud cackle of laughter and the door clicked open.

Poems about *Bertha*

Mr Dave Birtwhistle, now widowed is selling his boat to Justin and moving to a flat near to Limehouse Cut, in a boatyard where he was often berthed and where Justin will be moored. His grandson lives nearby. The task this week was to write poetry – so I wrote these two poems, expressing Dave's feelings about his beloved boat, Bertha.

Bertha Narrowboat

all those years

seasons of love

chugging quietly

slipping away

sliding along the cut

****

he smiles

admiring

her steady beat

lifesaver

lifegiver

****

he wonders

how

she will fare now – then

no longer

his

Bertha Mostly Berthed

window boxes ablaze

there she sits

a sturdy girl

in glossy seaweed green

curtained portholes

polished brass

****

sometimes

and with purpose

she chugs quietly

slicking dark ripples

through narrow channels

her engines thrumming

* ** ** ** *| .| .\|. .\|. **

not often heard now

on cold mornings

calls may rise in mist

check ropes there

and over here

for towed pontoons

of coal or wood or stone

Clara Left Behind/ Den Taking Root

(Den is Justin's father, who has invited himself to stay with Clara and the children.)

He'd already put the house up for sale in Wimbledon. It was an inspired move, not the selling of the house in itself, but what to do with the funds. He'd like to build onto Jussy's and Clara's cottage, or even a lodge in the garden – one of those things that came kitted out, 'Dad's Pad', that's what he'd call it. They both needed him, it was pretty obvious, not to mention the twins. He hadn't quite decided when to tell them about it yet. He planned to wait for Jus to come home. Never knew if he was coming home, not until the last minute; there was a chance this coming weekend he might escape to Suffolk with the extended heatwave making London dustier than ever. He stopped in his tracks on the path through the woods. 'See. See', he grinned to himself, he was already calling this recent Suffolk base 'home.' Yes, it would ease everyone's problems, give him extra spending money, perhaps calm things down; so long as he had access to his stash when things got a bit tense and Clara didn't find out where he'd hidden the bottles of spirits. What with Clara being stubborn about moving and all, and her email business beginning to pick up; then to cap it all Jus buying the narrowboat. He hadn't seen that coming.

He'd looked back at the cottage from the gate; Clara was doing her thing. He'd seen her: she was at her window, probably having a restless time of it, checking there were treats in his pocket to give Arthur on his return. Didn't want to get Clara annoyed, waking her up, the state she was in.

The sun was gone now and there was this magical time between sunset and dusk, a pause, when the afterglow lit where it fell. High in the cathedral canopy birdsong echoed through the woods. Not for the first time he wished he'd brought his camera, come to that a sound recorder, but then grinned to himself. Hmm, might give the wrong impression.

Out of the woods, he strolled to a cottage on the far side of the green, knocking on the heavy lion knocker and was greeted, and entered. Much later, the air now cool, the sky inky, lit by a sliver of moon, he exited, the door closing quietly behind him as he made his way back towards the wood.

He found his torch to help him to keep to the path. There were night noises; he heard a vixen's cry some distance away, but it was a familiar route. Since he had been involved personally with some of the female inhabitants of the village through the calendar photography sessions, it turned out there were women who were looking for male company without any strings. He treated invitations of various kinds with equal enthusiasm and promptly forgot most encounters.

In that regard, there seemed to be a temporary misunderstanding between Liz and Mary. He'd fancied Liz from the off, in fact. They'd met up at the pub for a drink once or twice. She was a little reserved and he liked her for it. He'd asked her out for a meal a couple of times, which, he had to admit, was after he'd taken Mary for a drink with her son, who wanted to pursue photography at college. After that Liz was cool with him. Still, the other female members of the church who'd volunteered to be in the calendar seemed happy to contact him on his mobile. They'd all used his mobile when he was photographing, so any cancellations could be re-arranged quickly. Mary confided in him that Liz no longer wanted her company outside of work, and she missed her. Den found it difficult to believe it could be about him.

Still, Den was flattered and that night had gone into the spirits shed, when he was sure Clara had gone inside after watering the garden, taking out a bottle of Glenlivet to celebrate. The next morning he was hung over, glad the twins were getting the bus and didn't need a lift to school, so he used mouthwash and cleaned his teeth twice in case Clara got a whiff and had a go at him before going out to the workshop.

He did not want to be banished back to Wimbledon, particularly since he'd had an initial offer on his house, which was far in excess of what he'd expected. He certainly didn't fancy sharing the narrowboat with Jus, even temporarily, not that he thought there'd be an offer forthcoming. Also, he considered, with some modesty he thought, he was needed here in his son's absence to help out on several fronts: there were the twins for a start, who were missing their dad. Not less important, from his viewpoint, was that he knew his cooking was considerably better than Clara's and it meant they all ate at mealtimes and not when she thought to stop work, not that he'd risk telling her.

He needed to tread carefully. He'd already risked sharing his beer shed secret with Joe the computer whizz, who'd helped him stack logs to hide it. He was regretting that decision a bit. Joe turned up more than Den had expected. Sometimes Clara joined them on the long seat outside the shed, where they'd chew the cud over anything that came to mind and watch the evening advance with the whirling, tiny bats out for insects as dusk fell. He'd have to start asking for a sub. Clara didn't seem to question when or where he got his supplies, must assume he picked it up randomly. If only she knew; he'd had a delivery when she'd gone with Jus to the hospital weeks ago. Still, they were having fun and a beer on summer evenings in the garden, with perfumes from the flowers and herbs around them adding to the atmosphere.

Yes, a permanent move was obvious. It was going to be such a gas!

A significant place linked to a journey

(This was one of the few tasks that Margaret didn't adapt to make it into part of the novel. It's a lovely piece, inspired by a place that obviously had quite an impact on her.)

Often it might rain, drifting sideways; a mist, I remember they called it. There were walks, big brave stridings out to be had, with backpacks; or before coffee a level stroll in a welcome thin sun along the edge of everything. Everything first dipping away, down to a rushing stream, bounding over rocks, then soaring to treeless wonders of high tors, their narrow paths marked by granite, lacing elegantly out of sight.

Except in winter, sheep dotted the distant places and shepherds rode out on horseback to check their livestock.

In the hamlet, all grass was short, nibbled by the donkey and occasional visiting black steer, who, looking up, uninterested, wandered off to quieter places.

There were two journeys to this place. I saw it first when I was eleven. We arrived in mist; there were no views, no people. It seemed a mystical place. We wandered around a little. Admired low stone walls, the tiny old church behind the cottages, then stumbled, wet and hungry back to our travelling caravan and Hillman Minx, for sandwiches and tea made on a primus.

Twenty years or so later I was there again, this time visiting my husband's family with our baby boy. I had heard so much about this place, where he had spent time in the war, rabbiting, working alongside an aunt on the allotment in the valley, and being free after the local school closed because the teachers were away fighting. I stood on the green. Only then did I realize I already knew this place. Its name, when I was eleven had escaped me.

It was then and is now a favourite place; sanctuary from other things. I need to touch the stone walls, admire the settled moss; hear water racing down from the tor; hear birds; mostly hear the ghosted laughter of distant holidays.

For years I rarely visited; but I am back and it hasn't changed: unlike almost everything else.

Jennie Colton

Jennie is a particularly important member of the group, as she's in charge of the coffee order. She's incredibly modest about her writing, yet every week, she produces a beautifully finished piece that entertains and often moves us. Ed.

A Village Affair

This short story was inspired by a real incident during a performance many years ago at a Cheddar Stage Society pantomime. I was on stage when the embarrassing 'exposure' happened; just like Marjorie in the story, the lady in question carried on like a real trouper, for the rest of that night and the two nights that followed. Unlike Marjorie, however, she never took part in a Stage Society pantomime again!

Definitely Not A Sonnet

The title says it all! Despite our task for the week being to write a sonnet, I realized after several increasingly desperate attempts to do the homework that Shakespeare really was a genius and this was a task beyond my poetry-writing capabilities.

The Unexpected Visitor

We had been asked to write a piece on how we would feel if we met someone famous from the past, and as we are all scribblers, I imagined what it would be like if a famous author turned up to one of our classes.

A Village Affair

The Lower Marsham Drama Group were in disarray. Every year they had entertained the village with pantomimes and plays but this year there was disagreement among the ranks. Marjorie Fortescue, the Drama Club Chairman and leading light in the society, thought it was time to have a change, and that instead of the usual format, they should try something different and do a Gilbert and Sullivan operetta.

After the howls of 'no way' and 'we haven't got any proper singers' had died down, Marjorie pressed on with her idea, blithely ignoring the protests. "After all," she thought, "there isn't anyone else who can direct, so without me they're stuffed!"

She didn't voice this treacherous thought out loud but only smiled sweetly and in her most persuasive and charming manner, set about trying to change everyone's mind. Of course she succeeded, although there was some disgruntlement amongst several of the group. They stubbornly refused to agree, but when it came to the vote, Marjorie won.

The next task was to decide which of the operettas to choose. Secretly, Marjorie had always fancied herself as a bit of a singer and having thoroughly rescarched the plots, she decided that 'Iolanthe' was the one to choose. She imagined herself in a beautiful, gauzy fairy costume and although the character was supposed to look about seventeen, Marjorie decided that with a bit of make-up and a long blonde wig she could easily look the part.

Her choice was met with some incredulity by the other club members, especially when she announced that not only would she be directing the thing, she would be taking on the leading role and that auditions for the other parts would be held in a few days.

Auditions bordered on the disastrous. The few stalwarts who turned up appeared to be incapable of singing in tune, but Marjorie was not to be deterred, and with much flattery and cajoling, she persuaded the poor unfortunates to take on the roles for which they were wholly unsuited.

Rehearsals proved very trying. Marjorie was a hard task master and made her cast repeat their songs over and over again. She had bullied her poor unfortunate husband, Robert, into playing the piano accompaniment, making the next few weeks a torment for him at home as well as at rehearsals. But gradually, to her credit, the operetta began to take some sort of shape, although the performances were well below the Drama Club's usual mediocre standard.

The next thing to organise was costumes for the cast. The group had several ladies who could always be relied upon to produce whatever was needed but on this occasion, Marjorie decided that she would make her own. She pictured herself floating across the stage in a shimmer of pale green gossamer, singing like an angel. She could already see the front cover of the local village paper, fulsome in its praise of her talent.

As the day of the dress rehearsal arrived, the cast, by now still barely adequate for the task that had been thrust upon them, were a little surprised when Marjorie turned up in a sweat shirt and jogging trousers, while they were all trussed up in their appropriate costumes.

"My costume isn't quite finished," she informed them, "but rest assured it will be ready for our first night tomorrow."

The dress rehearsal was a nightmare. Marjorie, although able to warble in tune, was not leading lady operetta material, but seemed oblivious to her shortcomings, and as the evening progressed the rest of the cast became more and more despondent. Marjorie dismissed their worries by saying that dress rehearsals were nearly always bad and that things would be alright on the night.

As the audience trickled into the hall the next evening, there was the usual buzz of expectant murmurings, which grew louder as people bought their drinks and settled themselves in their numbered seats to await their entertainment. The village shows had always been popular and well supported but not everyone was as enthusiastic about Gilbert and Sullivan, so ticket sales were well down. Being aware of this, Marjorie had exerted the full force of her personality on the hapless choir master of the church, practically ordering him to bring along the choir members to this musical soiree.

The lights dimmed and Robert played the first bars of the music as the curtains slowly drew apart. The beginning of the operetta did not go well. Several characters forgot the words and needed prompts, more difficult to do than with just the spoken word. The short dance routines were chaotic, causing someone from the audience to shout out that 'they looked more like fairy elephants than fairies'. Undeterred, Marjorie waited in the wings, resplendent in her fairy costume and ready to take the audience by storm.

When the cue for her to come on was given, she burst onto the stage in a cloud of pale green. There was an audible gasp from the audience, followed by an instant of absolute silence before the entire audience burst out into gales of hysterical laughter. What Marjorie hadn't realised was that her costume was completely see-through from the waist down so that the voluminous white knickers, that covered her not so small, not very fairy-like bottom, were exposed in the glare of the spotlight. Unaware of the cause of the audience's great mirth, she carried on regardless and it wasn't until the interval that the full extent of her exposure was revealed to her by the other cast members.

But Marjorie was not a woman to be put off easily and she carried on with the rest of the performance, ignoring the loud chortles that greeted her every appearance on stage. At the end of the show, as the cast took their bows, the loudest, most raucous applause was given to Marjorie.

The following performances over the next couple of evenings found the hall packed. Marjorie came on stage in her see-through costume on both occasions, having realised that her exposure was helping to swell the numbers. She was not even upset when the local paper described the show as 'Pants'.

"Next year," she thought, "I think we might try a proper opera. I've always fancied playing Carmen..."

Definitely Not a Sonnet!

My task was to write a sonnet,
Fourteen lines of ten syllables each,
So I racked my brains hard
Tried to think of the Bard
But inspiration proved out of reach.

'Try love', that's a popular topic
I can't fail with affairs of the heart
But my muse had left town
And I felt so let down
And completely unable to start.

I really enjoy writing stories.
Romances, who-dunnits, short tales.
I'm a sucker for prose
But intelligence goes,
With verse and all it entails.

So I thought I'd leave it to Shakespeare,
Or Tennyson, Byron or Keats
I'm sure they'd not mind
I just know they'd be kind
Though my sonnet's a bit of cheat!

The Unexpected Visitor

Sue entered the small building known as the barn, which was located in the carpark of a local hostelry, and switched on the light. It felt chilly inside, even though the room was windowless and the walls thick, so she put the heaters on to warm it up before the ladies arrived.

The class was supposed to start at 10.30am, but since all her pupils were pretty much 'ladies of leisure' and their participation entirely for interest rather than necessity, they tended to drift in around the designated start time and were not always as prompt as they could have been.

Once they were all seated around the large table that dominated the room, the usual discussions, about every topic you could think of, began. Conversation flowed animatedly and often continued long after the coffee arrived. Sue struggled heroically to stem the flow of rhetoric and to try and instil some kind of order into the proceedings, because, after all, the class was supposed to be a creative writing class, and she could see all her plans for the session having to be shelved yet again until the following week.

Finally, she announced that enough was enough and it was time to get down to some writing, but before that, the ladies could read their homework out to the group for constructive criticism. Just as Margaret was about to begin reading the next chapter of the book she was writing, the door was suddenly opened and a young woman, clothed in what looked very much like fancy dress, walked in. Her dress was long and full and rustled as she moved and over it she had a short cloak fastened at the neck. But most extraordinary of all was the pretty flowery bonnet on her head, tied on with blue ribbon around her chin.

"Oh hello," said Sue. "Can we help you? Are you from the Kings of Wessex – but it's not Charities Week...." Sue's voice faltered as she tried to think why this young woman would be dressed in such a manner.

"My name is Jane," said the young woman, "and I've come from Bath to visit Cheddar Gorge – it's talked about at various afternoon teas at the spa as a beautiful place to see and so I thought I would visit, perhaps to give me inspiration for a new novel. We stopped at this tavern to take refreshment and the landlord kindly told me that there were ladies in the barn who were authors. It's so difficult for ladies to be authors, is it not? I have had to get my novels published through my brother. Do you not find that it is not really considered seemly for a woman to be an author?"

Sue and the ladies were too astonished to speak and sat for several seconds open mouthed. Was this woman for real? Was it some silly practical joke? Finally, having recovered sufficiently to begin to think the unthinkable, Julie asked what her full name was.

"My name is Jane Austen," she said " and I'd love to hear some of your stories. May I sit down? After you've read me your work perhaps you would be so kind as to give an opinion on my latest novel."

With that, she gracefully swished her skirt to one side so she could sit on the only free chair, then removed her bonnet, carefully placing it on the table. The ladies all felt very self-conscious reading their stories but Jane kindly nodded as each finished, although she expressed her confusion at some of the plots, as she couldn't understand how it all seemed so different from her own experience of life.

"Now I shall read you the first chapter of the novel I've just finished. It's about a genteel family, who have very little money and five daughters to find husbands for."

Then she reached into the pocket of her dress and pulled out a small book and began to read the words familiar to all the ladies in the room:

"*It is a truth universally acknowledged, that a single man in possession of a good fortune must be in want of a wife...*"

When she had finally finished reading, she looked shyly around and asked what everyone thought of her story.

"I think of it almost as if it were my baby, it is my favourite of all the novels I have written. But do you think it is any good – will it be successful? We do need more income now that Father has died."

Sue stood up, moved across to where Jane was sitting and took her hand.

"I can assure you," she said, "that your book will become a classic, read by millions of people – and you will be considered one of the greatest authors in English literature."

Jane blushed modestly. Then she slowly stood up, picked up her bonnet and fastened it under her chin and placed her book back in her pocket.

"It has been a pleasure to meet fellow lady authors," she said "and thank you so much for your kind words. I have to go now, it will take some time to return to Bath." And with that she walked quietly out of the room.

"Well ladies," said Sue. "After all that excitement, we've just got time to do a short piece of prose or poetry, describing how you would feel after meeting a famous person."

And as the words left her lips, the only sound in the room was that of five pens gliding furiously over five sheets of paper.

The Solace of Winter

Lorna hastily thrust her front door key into the lock and bustled inside, glad to get out of biting east wind. It had been an upsetting day for her.

"Why are winter funerals so much more depressing than summer ones?" she thought. But at least the rain had held off, although the clouds looked more threatening than before.

The days were short now and at just after four o'clock, dusk was beginning to fall. She took off her coat and hung it on the peg in the hall, then went into the lounge debating whether she should draw the curtains to shut away the world outside. She felt very sad; the father she had loved and looked after in his declining years had died suddenly from pneumonia and today she had said her final goodbye to him. The house felt lonely and a lump rose in her throat as she looked at the armchair next to the fire where he'd sat every evening, and she realised it would always be empty from now on.

Trying to pull herself together, she walked over to the window and noticed that the light outside had changed silently and almost imperceptibly. Tiny flakes of snow began to fall from the bloated grey-white clouds. She stood transfixed as the flakes became bigger and more frantic, tossed chaotically by the force of the wind. It seemed to Lorna that they were almost dancing. She marvelled as some of the flakes hit the window and she could see that they looked like tiny lace doilies, beautiful and delicate.

Someone had once told her that no two snowflakes were ever the same, she remembered. Could that be possible?

She stood and gazed for a long time, hypnotised and somehow cheered by the dancing snow as it slowly began to cover the ground in a blanket of white. She was just about to finally close the curtains when thoughts of the day came flooding back After the cremation, she had wandered through the gardens surrounding the crematorium, wanting to be alone to feel her grief. She had been strangely consoled by the sight of the great clumps of snowdrops that were springing up all around the bare trees – new life promised after the bleakness of winter. Her father had always planted snowdrops in his garden before he became too elderly to cope in his own home. He'd marvelled that such tiny delicate flowers, like little white bells, could flourish year after year and push their way through the frost-hardened soil,

"I shall plant snowdrops," she resolved. "They'll be a lovely reminder of Dad."

Closing the curtains briskly, she went out into the kitchen to make herself a drink.

"I've had enough sherry for one day," she thought. "I need hot chocolate." And she set about making the milky, soothing drink.

Clutching the warm mug in her hands, she settled herself down in her chair and breathed in the sweet aroma of the hot chocolate. Then, raising her mug in the gesture of a toast, she whispered:

"Here's to you Dad. Love you always."

Angela Cornborough

Angela is a talented artist and craftsperson, as well as being a dab hand at writing. Her stories often have an unexpected twist at the end, and are haunting in more ways than one. Ed.

I have always enjoyed writing stories, right from when I was very young. I have no particular style or genre; I just write whatever comes into my head.

These stories were inspired by prompts from the writing group.

Moving On

The removers came on the Tuesday afternoon to start packing. Sam didn't want to leave the house but found he had no say in the matter. Fifty-five years he'd lived here, all his married life. Downsizing they called it and he could see that it made sense, but he still didn't like it. Agnes was very stoic but he could tell she was finding it hard too. She found everything hard these days. She got confused easily – one minute she was fine, the next she didn't know what day it was.

"Yes," Sam thought, "I can see why the children thought this was the best thing to do."

He didn't like the removers touching their things, wrapping up books, pieces of china, even his collection of pipes, with no sentimentality. These objects meant nothing to them, he reasoned, just another job, another family to move on. Memory by memory his life was being packed away and stacked up in a corner to await the furniture van. However had they accumulated all this stuff? It was a bit different from when they moved in, he remembered. Two odd armchairs, a table, a bed, wardrobe and dressing table and a few cardboard boxes; most of it second-hand, donations from the rest of the family to get them started.

He remembered that day so clearly. Agnes had been so pretty: beautiful blonde hair, a real English rose complexion, a trim little figure – oh, she was lovely. He'd never looked at another girl after he'd met her. 'A girl in every port' for a sailor they said, but not for him. She was his one and only. She'd worn very well, he admitted; a little bit thicker round the middle maybe, and her hair had lost a lot of its lustre, but she was still in pretty good shape for her age. He'd carried her, his new bride, over the threshold that first day, almost dropping her while they negotiated the turn through the inner door, laughing, full of joy, their lives ahead of them. Where had the time gone?

The removers were efficient, he had to admit. The living room was cleared in no time, sad and forlorn in its emptiness, the brighter patches where the pictures had hung standing out starkly, the indentations in the carpet where the sofa had stood still evident. Early spring sunshine streamed through the huge bay window, bouncing multi-coloured beams back off the stained glass cupboard doors in the alcoves, highlighting the carving on the oak doors beneath, darkened by years of polish. They were pew ends from a dismantled church, he'd been told when they bought the house, and for some reason he'd found that reassuring. It was a lovely room – a lovely house – Edwardian, with all the period features still in place. The sunlight showed how shabby the room had become though; the yellowing, chipped paintwork, the faded wallpaper peeling at the corners and thick layers of dust everywhere. It hadn't been decorated for he couldn't remember how many years and neither he nor Agnes had realised how bad it was till now. The new people would come in and rip it all out anyway, he suspected; they wanted bright, modern interiors, easy to keep clean, trendy. He and Agnes liked it as it was; traditional.

They'd been so happy here.

On Wednesday, they came to take the furniture, tramping up and down the stairs, treading dirt into the carpets. Agnes had always been a most particular housekeeper, but now she didn't seem to care – he wondered if she even noticed. He wandered listlessly through the house for a last look before everything was moved, trying to imprint the images into his memory, his heart heavy. The packers seemed to be everywhere; filling boxes, carting furniture out to the van, joking with each other or whistling as they worked, while Agnes was forever in and out offering tea and biscuits. They were very patient with her, politely refusing, saying they needed to get on, tight schedule and all that. Sad to think you could pack someone's life into a few boxes and take it away in a van. He left the packers to it and went out into the garden to find some peace.

He'd always loved the view over the wall – it was one of the things which had attracted them to the house in the first place. It was a pity you couldn't see the suspension bridge from here, but he supposed you couldn't have everything. The house was on a ridge on one side of the gorge and looked out across the city on the other side. The river, much narrower here than at its mouth where it brought life to the town, threaded its way sinuously through the bottom of the valley. The railway line kept company, following its route arrowlike, missing out the twists and turns, parting company only when it plunged into the inky darkness of the tunnel. It was only leisure craft that frequented this reach of the river these days;

narrow boats awash with tourists, the occasional motor boat and the university rowing club, which had its boat house just upstream; the water slid by serenely, unaware of the watcher above.

The smoke and sparks belched out from the old steam trains as they thundered past had once kept the vegetation on the slope under control, but since their demise it had become a tangled mess of scrub and bramble which threatened to invade the garden – a losing battle he had ceased fighting many years ago. Time was when he used to tie one end of a rope round his waist, the other round the apple tree and lower himself down the steep bank to hack it all back with a machete, while Agnes flapped about in the garden convinced he would plunge to his death on the railway line a hundred feet below – nothing more than a Pyrrhic victory, but even that was denied to him now. A hot air balloon bobbed up from behind the trees on the far side of the gorge, a huge grinning face, mocking him for his melancholy. He watched, mesmerised, until a whoosh, as a tongue of flame licked upwards into the body, brought him back to earth.

It was that funny time of day – not quite dark, but not really light – when the world stands still for a moment, half-way between waking and dreaming. The lights of the city began to wink into life on the other side of the gorge and he noticed the red ribbon of car lights as the traffic built up in the evening rush hour. It was odd to see all those cars and imagine the noise on the other side – here there was no more than a soft hum, everything was peace and tranquillity, as if the world had stopped breathing, disturbed only by the occasional call of a bird settling down for the night. A light mist was beginning to roll in across the river meadows, shrouding the trees eerily, intensifying the feeling of unreality he felt out there in the garden. He shivered, let out a long, slow sigh and turned reluctantly back towards the house – he would miss all this.

He walked back through the darkening garden across the dew-sparkled grass, stopping now and again to touch a plant here and a shrub there; that one Agnes had brought home from a walk in the woods when they were on holiday one year, and this, one of the children had bought for Mother's Day. Daffodils peeped out from between the winter stems of spent perennials, not yet brave enough to fully expose their egg-yolk yellow blooms. It was fully dark by now and it was difficult to make anything out properly as he peered through the window into his workshop. It had been a while since he'd been able to do much in there; at one time, he'd seemed to spend every available minute mending broken toys and household paraphernalia, and he'd wistfully hoped his sons would want to keep some of his tools, if only for old-time's sake. Memories of happy days with his family crowded in on each other and tears threatened his eyes; he shook himself to dispel the gloom.

He knew he had to go, he really had no choice in the matter, but letting go and leaving was hard. He'd had a good life, but such a long time in one place, and now moving on to he didn't quite know what, frightened him. He hadn't seen the new place and couldn't imagine how everything would fit into a tiny two bedroom ground-floor flat. Bobby had taken Agnes to see it just after Christmas and she said it was just what she wanted. She didn't want to stay in the house; it was too much for her now. He understood, but it saddened him.

The removers had almost finished by the time he went back inside. Agnes was making more tea while Bobby, Kathy and Sean finished off last minute cleaning and tidying. There was a flurry of activity as the electricity and gas people came to read the meters and then unnatural silence. Nothing remained of his life; everything he possessed was now in the furniture van on its way north. Bare light bulbs in every room, and street lamps shining in through curtainless windows, cast eerie shadows on the walls. Each room still held its memories and in his mind's eye he revisited times gone by, the happy ones making his heart ache with longing. He wanted to scream out loud *I don't want this to happen*, he wanted the years to wind back, for him and Agnes to be starting out afresh. He would willingly take all the bad times again for the sake of the good. He was not a man prone to tears, men of his generation didn't cry, but he had to wipe moisture from his eyes and cheeks just the same. The house began to settle, making the creaks and ticks he had grown so used to over the years; sounds that comforted him at night with their familiarity. It began to grow cold.

Bobby appeared with the last box – tea-making

paraphernalia, inevitably – to stow away in the car. He, Kathy and Sean muffled Agnes up in a coat and walked her round the house to say her goodbyes. Sam watched, her frailty evident as she struggled with the stairs. He wondered what she was thinking; it was difficult to tell these days. There were no tears, just a last lingering look, a sigh, and then she was gone.

Bobby came back, supposedly to check everything was turned off, but really for one final moment of silent contemplation in his childhood home. With a shrug of the shoulders a few swift strides took him to the door. The door slammed, the key turned in the lock and the ring of Bobby's footsteps echoing on the flagstone path faded away.

Sam wanted to follow but knew he could not. His place was only in their hearts now. He heard the car pull away and watched, as everything he had ever loved disappeared into the night.

The Abbey Vaults Hotel

The building was unbelievable: very *Gormenghast*, doubtless with a mad woman lurking in the attic. The drive was long and lined with trees and shrubs: a riot in spring and summer for sure but now, in the depths of winter, almost sinister – dark, wet and broody. A figure stood by the roadside and we locked eyes as I passed. Another delegate out for a constitutional, I mused.

I wasn't really looking forward to the weekend. There had been a sudden summons from work to attend a conference as the original attendee had been struck down with some mysterious illness. I had planned a girlie weekend with some friends – I'd been looking forward to it.

The Abbey Vaults Hotel was opulence itself; a circular reception area, with a *Gone with the Wind* staircase winding to the upper storey. Highly polished wood reflected the chandeliers and made the floor look almost liquid.

My room was on the ground floor, overlooking the parkland, and I wasn't surprised to see the ruins of a small ecclesiastical building in the near distance. I decided it needed investigating as soon as I'd unpacked. It would be good to get some exercise after the long journey.

A leaflet in reception told me that the hotel had once been attached to a Cistercian Abbey so I wrapped up against the cold and set off across the lawn.

"I hadn't realised it was so cold," I said to the receptionist as I picked up my key on returning. There was some old chap out there without a warm overcoat – just looking at him chilled me to the bone. I think I need a warm fire and a cup of tea." The receptionist went pale and looked anxious.

"What did he look like?" she asked, almost in a whisper.

"Well, he was dressed quite oddly really; like an old-fashioned cleric – you know, long black frock coat, white starched shirt with a tie front, tall black hat – the works. Lord knows how long he's been out there, I'm sure I passed him on my way down the drive. He must be perishing, though he didn't show any signs of it."

The manager had appeared from nowhere and was listening intently. The two exchanged glances.

'Did you speak to the … gentleman?' asked the manager.

"I said good evening as we passed and he tipped his hat – why?" Another exchange of looks.

"I think perhaps it might be better if you stayed away from there, Madam. I'll look into it," he answered, avoiding my question.

"Oh he was quite harmless, I'm sure," I replied. "I was concerned for his well-being, that's all."

"Perhaps so, but I would still counsel you to keep to the hotel, or at least not to go out unaccompanied."

"Very well," I huffed, thinking they were making a big fuss about nothing. But perhaps they'd had trouble with him in the past.

As the evening wore on, the weather worsened. Snow flurries started as it got dark and by the time I went to bed there was a good covering on the ground. It looked quite ghostly from my bedroom window. I was spellbound by the almost sinister beauty of the view. I moved closer to the window. I was sure I had seen something move among the abbey ruins. A deer probably, I thought, trying to convince myself I had not seen a black clad figure.

My dreams were disturbing and I slept fitfully. Despite the comfort and warmth of the bed, I shivered slightly. I rose as daylight started to filter through the curtains and felt compelled to look outside.

Snow lay thick all around and everywhere was still, all sound muffled and distorted. I strained my eyes for movement in the abbey but there was nothing. I jumped back in fright as a bird crashed into the window, a ragged black crow. It must have broken its neck, poor thing, for it fell to the ground and never moved again.

The morning was taken up with presentations and meetings – deadly dull but apparently vital to the company's well-being. I was desperate to stretch my legs and get some air. I donned my coat and despite a small pang of guilt at reneging on my promise not to go out alone, I set off down the path.

It was so cold that the very air itself had frozen and rainbow droplets were scintillating all around me. It was like being in another world. I kept carefully to the cleared paths and was not overly surprised to find the elderly gentleman approaching from the opposite direction. A shiver went through me when I thought of the manager's reaction but I brushed it aside. Good lord, the man looked barely strong enough to carry himself, let alone to do me any harm.

As he drew near I couldn't help but ask: "Do you not feel the cold?" I reached out and touched him lightly on the shoulder. I withdrew my hand with a jerk as I felt a terrible force I couldn't explain go through me. He lifted his eyes to mine. They were dark and fearsome and I looked away quickly. He gave a slight bow and moved on. I found I was sweating despite the cold, which seemed to be intensified by his presence. I turned and headed back to the safety of the hotel as fast as I could.

I would have liked some brandy but knew it wouldn't do for someone to smell it on my breath in the middle of the day. I ordered an Irish coffee instead and sat as close to the fire as I could. I would definitely not be venturing out again until I left for good.

The manager came over to me and asked if I was all right and I realised I was shivering despite the fire.

"Just cold," I lied. "I foolishly took a little walk ... needed some air ..." I trailed off feebly. The manager paused before asking:

"Did you ... see anyone while you were out? The clerical gentleman for instance?" I blushed, knowing he had caught me out in my lie.

"Yes, I ... erm ... I did bump into him."

"Did you speak to him, or ..." and he hesitated just a fraction too long – "or ... touch him?"

"I was worried that he was cold. I may have touched him on the shoulder. What is it you're not telling me?" I blurted out.

"Nothing, nothing – he's just an undesirable ... being and it's best not to interact with him. He may feel he has made some connection to you. There is – how shall I put it – a darkness about him."

"Oh, don't be so theatrical! I'm sure he doesn't mean any harm."

"And yet you are trembling."

"Just gave me a bit of a fright, that's all,' I said, as brightly as I could, trying to convince myself as much as him.

"Please, promise me that you will not leave the hotel again." His expression was so grave and I so unnerved that I agreed readily and knew that this time I meant it.

"I will arrange for your things to be moved to an upper room,"

"There's no need for that," I insisted. "It's only one more night. He's not likely to break in, is he?" The manager was not happy but spread his hands and sighed in resignation. I couldn't wait for the next evening when I could go home.

The afternoon passed in a daze. I kept feeling the shock when I touched the old man. My heart raced every time and it took all my resolve to calm myself once more.

I could eat no dinner that evening but finally had my brandy and felt much better for it. "Stuff and nonsense," I upbraided myself. "Pull yourself together." I retired early, inexplicably exhausted.

I made a hot drink, I watched the news, I read, I tossed and turned, but sleep would not come. I paced the floor, willing myself not to look out of the window. Yet without knowing how, I found myself staring out into the beautiful moonlit night, searching the abbey ruins for signs of movement.

And there it was – a black clad figure. Was it beckoning? I turned away and backed into the corner, my pulse racing. My palms were sweaty, while my lips were dry. My breathing was ragged and I felt a sob catch in my throat.

Before I realised what I was doing, I was back at the window. The man seemed to draw me like a magnet. The moon shone fully on the figure now and there was no doubt about it, it was beckoning, calling me to go out and join it.

Maybe there was some rational explanation, I tried to reason with myself. Maybe there was something it wanted to tell or show me; a being from another dimension that had unfinished business. Maybe he'd been murdered and wanted to show me where his body had been hidden. I laughed at my foolishness but was convinced nonetheless by the inevitability of this truth.

Without thinking I dressed rapidly – a long black skirt, white high neck blouse and black shawl – where had these clothes even come from? They certainly weren't mine. I refused to think about it and slipped on my little boots – not really suitable for the weather conditions, but I was so eager to get to the bottom of the mystery that I didn't given them a second thought.

I ran through the hotel foyer and was hailed by the night porter.

"Madam! Please don't go out there, it's not safe!" I waved his warning aside and headed for the door. He leapt from behind the desk and tried to intercept me but I was already through. I heard him speaking urgently into the phone as I raced out into the freezing night air.

"Does anyone know what happened?" asked the police inspector.

"We tried to warn her but she wouldn't listen," said the hotel manager. "He's abroad again …" There was a sharp intake of breath from the inspector and the small group of staff looked from one to the other and nodded silently.

As I had feared, there was a body. I was just surprised to find that it was mine.

The Temple Of The Four Winds

Alice had climbed the hill every Sunday for the past seventy years, arriving at the folly as near to four o'clock as she could make it. In her youth she had made the ascent at a run, but as time went on, her feet began to drag and now it took her an age.

The folly was a Greek Temple, dedicated to the four winds. It stood at the top of the hill and the ground fell away sharply on the other side. At the bottom, beneath the temple, a small semi-circular lake hugged the hillside and paths meandered through wooded parkland. The trees here were broad-leaved, natural, untamed, whereas the trees above were obviously planted, each one of uniform height, shape and size. When they were in full leaf they resembled enormous lollipops, so perfect was their roundness. But now, in late autumn, they were bare and stark.

It was quiet up here; the slightest of breezes made the trees sough. The smell of coal and wood fires rose from the houses down in the town and this mixed with the pungent smell of rotting leaves.

A mist had begun to fall and as the dying sunlight hit the trees they seemed to catch fire. A streak of gold shot across the grass to one side in a last attempt to stave off the inevitable darkness.

It grew cold and Alice shivered. She drew her collar up around her neck and settled her scarf a little higher. A waft of perfume tickled her nose – *Midnight in Paris* – Joe's favourite; she only wore it on Sundays.

Alice and Joe had met at a dance during the war. She hadn't wanted to go but Gladys persuaded her; and there he was. Not handsome, exactly but perfectly acceptable all the same. His nose was a bit too big and he had a wonky smile which lit up his face and made his eyes sparkle and crinkle at the corners.

"Would you like to dance?" he'd asked shyly. He was a Geordie; she had liked his accent. Alice had blushed and said nothing. She'd stood up and taken his hand and they'd danced all night. She learned that he had just been called up and was still doing basic training. She let him walk her home and they stood awkwardly at the gate while he plucked up the courage to kiss her. She blushed again, though she didn't resist. His mouth was warm, soft and sweet.

"Can I see you again?"

"If you want to."

"I certainly do," he laughed, and he spun her round.

They met on Sunday, had a picnic in the park and then climbed the hill to the Temple of the Four Winds. It became their place and when he told her he was being posted they agreed she would go to the Temple every Sunday at four o'clock and he would meet her there as and when he could. He promised he would come back for her but in her heart she knew he never would.

Sunday after Sunday Alice climbed the hill but Joe never came. Eventually she resigned herself and got on with her life as best she could.

She took in evacuee children and refugees and every Sunday she would march them to the top of the hill where they picnicked and played, never questioning why they did it. After the war, she adopted three of the children who had been orphaned and was content enough. As teenagers, they rebelled at the weekly jaunt, so she left them at home and climbed the hill alone once more. Now the children were long grown with children, and even grandchildren, of their own, but still Alice kept her vigil.

The grass was bejewelled with dew now and Alice could feel the wet seeping into her shoes. She stopped to rest by a tree, leaning against its rough trunk, trying to take strength from its solidity. She looked up towards the Temple, which was fast disappearing into the thickening mist. She realised she wasn't going to make it to the top; she had made her last visit. A small, hot tear traced the lines down her face. She fished out a handkerchief and wiped it away. She turned one last time, blew a kiss towards the Temple and whispered her goodbyes. She gave a melancholy sigh, pushed herself reluctantly away from the tree and readied herself for the descent.

A movement caught the corner of her eye and she half turned to see what it was. An indistinguishable shape – a deer probably, Alice thought – was moving up on the hillside. It held her spellbound and she watched as it moved towards her at a leisurely pace and eventually coalesced into the figure of a man. She held her breath, in anticipation rather than fear. It couldn't be surely; not after all these years! The figure drew level with her and stopped.

"Haway, bonnie lass!"

"Joe?" He hadn't changed at all; that ridiculous haircut that made his hair stick out at all angles, the over-large nose and the smile. His eyes sparkled and crinkled as he watched her. "Joe, is it really you?"

"Why aye lass; were you waiting for someone else?"

"N-no … but, what are you doing here?"

"I said I'd come back for you, now didn't I?" Alice smiled. It was true. "Well, here I am." He took her cold hand in his.

"Oh Joe, I've missed you!"

"I know bonnie lass, but everything's alright now." His kiss was just as sweet as she remembered.

They walked hand-in-hand up the hill, the climb as easy as it had ever been, to the Temple of the Four Winds. As they sat and watched the sun set, Joe put his arm round her and she nestled into him – happy and at peace in her last resting place.

Sally Green

Sally is the most recent addition to our group. She arrived saying she was particularly interested in writing for children, but she shows a distinct talent at writing for older audiences too. Over to Sally. Ed.

In 2018 I attended a writing workshop given by Sue as part of the Cheddar Arts Festival. I so enjoyed the session. For a long time, I have been interested in stories and words. Sue invited me to her weekly writing class to 'test the water'. I was swimming in the deep end from the first session. Such lovely people – I am continually learning and loving it.

I'm not sure where *The Life of a Jacket* came from. I suppose it stems from the interest and empathy I hold for people in different life situations; in the story I could engineer the situation to work out for the best – which is not always the case in real life.

The poem comes from an exercise where we were asked to list five places that were important to us, and write about one of them. The place I chose is London during 1970-73, when I was training to be a nurse.

The Life of a Jacket

Part 1

Mary loved her clothes. She propped herself on her walking frame and fingered the garments. Some designer wear, some cashmere, some silk. They were a throwback to her earlier days of a high-flying career in a prestigious London law firm and a high society life style.

Mary's full name was Lady Mary Elizabeth Milton. Her husband, from whom she was divorced, had been Sir Edward Milton, a notable entrepreneur who became a politician. After a few years he was knighted for his contribution towards legislation to improve the financial rights of the charitable sector. They had made a stunning couple back in the day, being a sociable pair and often seen out and about around London. They were stylish and Mary had a knack of making either a flamboyant or a classic outfit look good. After their acrimonious divorce some years later, it was agreed that Mary should keep the flat in Kensington. It was a spacious flat with three bedrooms. Mary's god-daughter would sometimes come and stay, which was company for Mary. It was a ground floor flat with an impressive and well-maintained front door. This had recently been re-done with black gloss and well-polished brass door fittings. There were two stone pillars at the top of the three stone steps leading up from the pavement. It was an elegant entrance.

Mary had continued her career until she was 67, and it was

only three years later that whilst she was travelling on the Circle Line on the tube one morning she felt dizzy and faint. She managed to get off the train on to the platform at Sloane Square, but on the escalator she must have passed out as she woke up to find herself lying in a hospital bed. A young doctor was standing over her and he told her that unfortunately she had suffered a stroke.

Now six months on, she was still a feisty and determined woman. She was walking, albeit a bit skew-whiff a lot of the time. Her right arm and hand caused her difficulty with ordinary tasks and made them tricky or unsafe. Then there was the issue of what to wear. It had come down to comfortable trousers with elasticised waist bands and tops that were easy to get on with an uncooperative right arm. No more figure-hugging cashmere cardigans for her, or neat pencil skirts. She sighed as she stared into her long mirrored wardrobe. Valerie, her valued cleaning lady, had volunteered to help Mary 'have a clear-out' as she put it.

"Time all this lot went, Lady Mary. It's no good having it all hanging here, just gathering dust."

A large black bag was produced and in no time, dresses, blouses, cardigans and the like were folded and placed in the bag. Then there was the jacket with the fake emerald brooch. This had been a result of an extravagant moment in Rome when she and Edward travelled there for one of his important meetings. Once he was installed in his meeting she had hit the designer shops! Surely this jacket didn't have to go? But Valerie was not having any of Mary's sentimental nonsense and the jacket too was despatched into the black bag. What a sad sight Mary's wardrobe was now. She tapped the doors quickly shut with her left hand and asked Valerie if she would be kind enough to make her a cup of Earl Grey tea before she left to go home. Valerie was leaving early today to take the bag of clothes to the charity shop near her flat in Lambeth.

Mary slumped into the winged armchair, which sat in the bay window of her bedroom, thoughts of her past life going around in her head...

Part 2

Kelly was rushing. Kelly was always rushing. She had an appointment with Derek, the man at the job centre. He had arranged an interview for her and she needed to find out the address and hoped to get some tips on what she should say. Interviews were not her strong point, and she was hoping for some guidance.

It was raining; her ripped jeans and trainers were soaked from an unforgiving bus driving at speed through a puddle in the road as she waited to cross. She felt a dishevelled mess.

Kelly was 30 and life had become tough. Through her twenties she had been an auxiliary nurse until little Tommy arrived unexpectedly three years ago now and not long afterwards her partner, also unexpectedly, found someone else and left them. So Kelly's life became a complex web of overwhelming love for Tommy, finding the rent for their small, damp flat each week, juggling childcare as nursery payments were too expensive, and looking for work. It all seemed very bleak to her right now and she was trying hard not to pin all her hopes on the forthcoming interview. That's why she needed to see Derek; she must get it right this time.

She emerged from her appointment at the job centre marginally more confident about things than when she had gone in. Derek had given her some helpful tips and impressed upon her that she must be on time. What particularly attracted Kelly to this job and made it more important to secure it, was that it was a live-in position. Also the interviewer had been clear that there would not be a problem with Kelly bringing Tommy along, provided the child was not unruly.

She had fifteen minutes to spare before she had to collect Tommy from her friend Kath. She walked past the charity shop on her way home and decided to pop in. She thought she might find something to wear for the interview - she could hardly go as she was, she thought, looking down at her damp and rather dirty jeans and trainers. At speed she flicked through the hangers in the small size ladies section where she found a straight skirt, size 10. It would do nicely, she thought. She had some thick black tights that Kath had given her at Christmas and her old black boots would be ok too. Three pounds – she could afford that.

Despite her rush this morning she had grabbed her bill jar and borrowed £10 from it, a loan that she hoped she would be able to pay back. She went to the counter with the skirt and whilst waiting behind a lady buying some books for her granddaughter, Kelly spotted a jacket hanging on the 'just in' rack. It was navy with a green sparkly brooch on the collar and really quite stylish. Probably too expensive she thought, but it had really caught her eye and she only had her cagoule to wear for the interview. She stepped out of the queue to take a closer look. The label said £5 but this was crossed through with red pen and £3 stood out as the actual price along with *Special January Sale Item*, also written in red. Her size too – this was too good to be true! The items came to £6 so £4 could go back into the kitty for now and she would deal with the £6 deficit some other time. *If I do the jacket up, no-one will see my t-shirt underneath*, she thought to herself. She paid the charity shop assistant and left with a spring in her step, helped by the fact that her trainers had dried out.

The interview day arrived. She gave Tommy his breakfast cereal and got dressed in her new outfit. She stood on a chair in the bathroom to try and see herself in the small mirror above the basin, turning to try and get a glimpse of her side view. Yes, she mused, this will do very nicely. She hardly recognised herself.

The number 19 bus took them from Lambeth High Road to five minutes from their destination. They arrived at the correct address and Tommy counted the steps up: one, two, three. Then

Kelly picked him up so that he could lift the big brass knocker in the shape of a lion's head. He banged it twice.

They waited outside the door for what seemed like a long time, during which Kelly was becoming increasingly nervous. Eventually the door slowly opened. An elderly, grey haired lady stood there behind a walking frame. She was a little bent over but she had a welcoming smile as she invited them in to the big hall.

"This... er...this is Tommy and my name is Kelly," was all Kelly could blurt out as her nervousness got the better of her. "Well, how do you do Tommy?" the elderly lady said bending even more and extending her crooked left hand to shake his tiny one. "It is very good to meet you, thank you for coming to visit me."

"We came on the bus and we sat at the front upstairs", Tommy piped up. He had none of his mother's shyness.

The elderly lady turned to Kelly saying, "Now dear, if we are going to have a chat perhaps you wouldn't mind making us a pot of Earl Grey tea. I believe my cleaning lady, Valerie, has got some orange squash in for young Tommy here. You should find everything in the kitchen, just down the corridor. I'm afraid this right hand of mine is hopeless with a kettle so that would be a great help to me." At this request, Kelly immediately relaxed. She had something to do and the elderly lady seemed so welcoming, and her flat was lovely.

As she made her way to the kitchen she could hear the

elderly lady talking to Tommy in a gentle voice and asking him to escort her to the sitting room. He had no idea what she meant but he automatically took her debilitated right hand, she steered her frame with her left and they made their way together.

" Have you seen my Mummy's special sparkly green brooch?" Tommy announced proudly to the elderly lady.

"Indeed I have," said the lady, "indeed I have…"

There was a wry smile on her face as she whispered to him: "You know, Tommy, I think your Mummy and I are going to get along just fine…"

An important place

I boarded a ferry
And then a train
To the smoke and the city
Goodbye country lane

A dreamy young girl
No clue of the world
I stood on the brink
Of what life would hold

Seventeen and a half
No more than that
With home now behind me
I knew that was that

A huge nurses' residence
Nervous laughter and chat
The matrons awaiting
To quell all of that

My group yet to meet
Lists of rules still to learn
Our uniform issued
Little money to earn

This seemed not to matter
It was love at first sight
The smell of the hospital
The vigil at night

Black stockings and cape
Starched cap and stiff apron
A formal old kit
All part of vocation

But despite the attire
It was the sense of belonging

The excitement of learning
Was quite overwhelming

Good friendships were made
With laughter a plenty
Through good times and bad
Those bed pans to empty

Juniors' job every morning
With day hardly dawning
Thirty eggs on the boil
Vats of porridge a-calling

Scurrying round like a mad
thing
The tea to get round
'The glamorous medicine'
Was still to be found

Ah, injecting an orange
Now that was quite novel
The patients were spared
Any amateur wobble

Lots of potions and pills
Catheter bags overflowing
In Casualty now
Lots of coming and going

No place for fainthearted
It has to be said
Blood, sweat and tears
Now – 'Make that bed'

All the fluids, the wounds
The drips and the drains
I'd have made a good

plumber
Way back in those days

Those surgical theatres
They can be intense
Correct order of instruments
Remember – or else

The children, the elderly
The infectious, the drunk
Interesting characters
A shoe full of gunk

How quickly and swiftly
Those three years were done
No more a student
Qualification had come

Outside the big doors
Red buses keep running
The taxis and ambulances
They all just keep coming

'An important place'
It was London for me
Through rose tinted glasses
Now maybe I see

But whatever 'your' story
This dreamy young thing
Left home and experienced
What life could bring.

Penny Harden

When I sit down to write, if I'm lucky, the ideas for a task set by Sue seem to emerge spontaneously, as if the computer itself is the creator/director, and my role, the useful typist. At other times – well, it's a very different experience!

I find autobiographical writing and poetry composition particularly enjoyable and therapeutic. An example of my autobiographical writing is *The Nightmare Journey*. This experience, which had haunted me for many years, was fully exorcised through being able, finally, to set it down in writing.

In my story-telling I conjure scenes for the audience describing the protagonist's point of view, rather than having the story come direct from the protagonist. The story *Abduction*, and to a degree, *The Lost Boy*, are examples of this approach.

The two poems, *The Pattern Repeated* and *What Is Yellow?* come from observations of the cycle of life. The first poem refers to species seemingly far removed from our own human instincts and behaviours, the second to one with which we may more easily identify.

The Nightmare Journey

It had been an enjoyable evening, visiting a close teaching friend in Harpenden, catching up on all the news and revisiting times spent teaching together in Luton, prior to my move to Bedford. Whilst we'd kept in 'phone contact, we'd not met for some considerable time. Around nine-thirty, it was time to make my way home to Ampthill, in mid-Bedfordshire. Melanie, my daughter, would be there, although my husband had a parents' evening at his school in Buckinghamshire, so would be late home.

My friend suggested I take the shorter, motorway route, rather than the 'A' road home.

"It'll be much quicker, Penny, and you won't have to drive through Luton town centre,"
she said encouragingly. Luton, like many larger cities, and Home-County town centres, was an unsavoury place at night, due mainly to drink and drug problems. There'd been recent reports of lone women's car doors being pulled open at traffic lights, and bags snatched. The police had advised women to drive through it with locked doors until the problem was resolved. Having lived and worked for some years in-and-around Luton, I did know short-cuts which avoided the centre, but at night, these could feel equally threatening.

"Oh, maybe I will, Barbara," I said gratefully, as I drove off. But I knew I probably wouldn't. Luton, at night, was unappealing to me, but the M1 Northbound appealed even less with its thundering night-time lorries transporting goods to the Midlands and beyond; together with speeding cars and goodness knows what else. I've always been a motorway phobic, even though census studies consider them to be a safer means of travel. In the event of a crash, the numbers of vehicles and casualties involved seem considerably greater than those on minor roads. However, at the last minute, when approaching the junction, I thought, "Blow it Penny. It *will* be much quicker." Just two junctions ahead and I'd be home in well under an hour.

Apprehensively, I slid the car into the motorway lane and, after five short minutes, my spirits lifted considerably. "You are so silly, Penny. Why all the fuss?" I asked myself. The motorway was practically empty, and the full silvery moon in the night-time sky illuminated the broad road beautifully. I relaxed a little, reflecting on the evening's visit, on Barbara, and how happy she was: the meal she'd cooked for us, and our non-stop chatter. In no time at all I saw the welcoming Toddington services sign up ahead, which was my cue to exit. I made my way on to the slip road. The sign, "Woburn, Ampthill," provoked a sigh of relief. I remember clearly studying my rear-view mirror, and noting that no other vehicle was behind me. When I reached the give way markings at the top of the slope, no other vehicle was approaching from either side. Having double checked all was clear, in both directions, I pulled forward, then right, and stopped at the red traffic lights. Checking my rear view mirror, once again, I was the sole person waiting for the green light. Not surprising given that mid-Bedfordshire is the least populated area of the entire county. When the lights changed, I headed off confidently. I was beginning to feel a little jaded but looking forward to relaxing with a cup of tea, once home.

Suddenly, out of nowhere, an old cream car was hugging my rear bumper so closely that I couldn't even see the driver's face. Alarmed and angered by the tailgater's aggressive behaviour, I wondered if it was due to drink, drugs, or possibly both? On the ill-lit, empty dual carriageway, there was adequate room for over-taking, so why was I being harassed in this way? Suddenly, the car dropped back, and thinking quickly, I decided to try to read the number plate in order to report him. But the car pulled out violently, and the driver now alongside, began staring directly at me in a wild and menacing manner. Then, just as quickly, he pulled ahead and applied his brakes, attempting to make me do like-wise. My heart raced. Anger now turning to fear, I felt weak and vulnerable. But somehow I managed to pull out and overtake him, narrowly avoiding a collision. I increased speed and scanned the road for other cars; the police, anybody. But the long, poorly lit ribbon road was empty. An odd house visible every now and then, but set well back from the road, and cloaked in darkness. I decided I would not be forced to pull over, or stop my car, for this seemed to be what he wanted. The tactics he employed continued for a few more miles. Each time he pulled parallel to my car, the proximity was such that it was as though he were sitting right next to me, which was terrifying. He glared and mouthed at me intimidatingly. In response, I tried shouting, "What are you doing?" to no avail.

All I could register was his dark, menacing, staring eyes, and his light-coloured jacket or raincoat. He seemed illuminated, which on reflection, I realised, meant his interior light was on. I couldn't figure out where he'd come from, given the emptiness of the road when I joined it.

The dark empty road intensified my feelings of terror and desperation. If only someone could spot him and alert the police. Anyone who might bring this nightmare to an end! Eventually, we approached the dim lights of Westoning village which raised my hopes of help. I knew that a pub was situated on the main road, so decided I'd pull over, jump out, rush in, and beg for help. But this plan was soon dashed. The monster, tailgating once again, made the plan too risky. If I turned into the small, gloomy car-park, at the rear, I'd be trapped if he followed me, which I felt certain he would. On leaving the village, there was a small, off-set, roundabout to cross, followed by approximately half a mile of tree-lined, sharp z- bends, which needed to be negotiated with great care. I dreaded the ordeal of getting through these obstacles, but knew I would then be entering the larger, more densely populated, and better lit village of Flitwick; the penultimate village to home. I might spot a pedestrian, pull in to someone's drive perhaps, or even see a police car. I hoped that these thoughts might occur to the mad man too, perhaps persuading him to take flight. But, as I reached Westoning's exit roundabout, the maniac attempted to come alongside me, and tried to drive me into its curve, forcing me to stop. Inexplicably, at the last second, as my front wheel grazed the kerb, I managed to accelerate just sufficiently to foil this plan, and raced onward toward the z-bends. One or two cars did approach, then pass me, as I flashed my lights in desperation. But the drivers' responses were most likely those of anger or frustration at my perceived thoughtless actions, which provided no results. On arrival at Flitwick, I scanned the road, desperately searching for some means of help. But there was none. The driver, however, was keeping a safe distance. "Maybe," I prayed, "he'll stop this now, and go elsewhere." Briefly, I considered the final spurt home, to safety and sanctuary. This prospect helped me to regain strength. "You're nearly home now Penny. Just hang on a bit longer."

As I crossed Flitwick railway bridge, and was about to turn left on to Ampthill Road, I noted, thankfully, that he was no longer behind me. My heart leapt with relief. But then, my terror returned. There he was, a little way back, and still in pursuit. It was at that very moment that I lost all hope. For I realised that I wouldn't, after all, be able to turn into my home road. How stupid had I been even to consider the notion? If he followed me into my road, he would know where I lived. Melanie would be alone in the house. I'd be placing my daughter too, in a vulnerable position, and would be totally unable to defend either of us. He might drive off, unsure of who was within. He could then monitor the occupants' comings and goings, and return at a time best suited to his plans, whatever they might be. As I passed my road, I tried desperately to consider my options. At the centre of our small town there were only two routes out, both of which filled me with despair. One, winding, wooded and remote, led to Woburn, five miles away. The second road led to Bedford, six-to-eight miles away, but equally undesirable, for both were poorly lit and largely deserted. The Bedford Road had a small police-station just before the boundary of Ampthill. However, it was unmanned in the evenings. If police help was required by members of the public, they were advised to use the outside telephone, situated on the wall, adjacent to the station entrance. The single other alternative for police assistance was to drive to Bedford's main police-station. "I've had it, I'm defeated," I thought. On the brink of tears now, I was thoroughly exhausted, both physically and mentally. Whichever road I chose would present the impossible odds of arriving safely. "There's nothing for it," I thought despairingly. "I'm going to have to risk driving into Ampthill Police Station car-park, leaping out, and hammering on the door. Maybe someone *would* be inside, and perhaps my assailant wouldn't be aware that the station is closed at night? Maybe ... maybe ... but it was my only hope of salvation!

Sweeping in to the car-park, and leaving my car door wide open as I leapt out, I dared not study anything other than the path ahead of me, and the station door, a symbol of safety.

Pounding wildly on it, I screamed like a woman possessed; tears flowing uncontrollably down my cheeks. Petrified that I'd be grabbed from behind and dragged into the victor's car, to whatever fate awaited me, I was completely overwhelmed and exhausted when the door opened, and a concerned and sympathetic face studied mine, as I blurted out my story incoherently. I wanted her to come immediately. To catch the monster who had caused me so much distress, and who might now escape to do likewise to some other poor unfortunate. However, the kind policewoman encouraged me to sit, and calm down, then fetched me a glass of water. She proceeded to tell me her plan. She would follow my car home, at a distance, back to the town centre, and, should I spot the car concerned, I was to pull over and point it out to her. I was then to go on home while she took over. She, or a colleague, would contact me, probably in the morning, as she believed me presently unfit to provide an official statement. I arrived home, relieved to find Malcolm's car on the drive, but still I did not feel safe, uncertain as to the mad man's whereabouts.

The following morning the officer, together with a colleague, arrived as planned. I felt wholly inadequate due to my inability to provide a comprehensive and detailed description of the man, or the car number plate. I provided the barest of details: Old cream car, middle-aged, European male, cream coat or jacket. Dark, greased back hair, and dark staring eyes. The officers were sympathetic and supportive, explaining that this was common to initial investigations, due to victim shock. I was told that I'd probably be able to recall further details as time went by. But what I was told next truly distressed me. There had been several accounts of lone women being hounded at night, on the stretch of the M1 on which I'd travelled. The police were unsure if these, together with my experience, were linked to the murder of a young mother, whose body was found beside an orange motorway help 'phone. It was believed that she was murdered as she attempted to use the 'phone, whilst her young child remained secured, strapped in to the car-seat. Unbeknown to me, the police, via the media, had advised women against travelling alone in the region, at night, if they could possibly avoid it. As the weeks went by, there were reports that women were employing a safety tactic, whereby a partner would lie down, invisibly, on the back seat of a car. Should the woman driver feel endangered, the partner could pop up, and record the car, and assailant details, to assist a police search. To this day, I am unsure whether my assailant was caught, and/or whether he was also responsible for committing murder.

The Pattern Repeated

Nervous eyes, blind to the danger
Of creature there lurking so still and so slender.
The skill of its threading, ensures a beheading
Once trapped, and wrapped, in its silken cocoon.

Try as it may, the elasticated display will not loosen
Its hold. Gripped and controlled. Now, struggling prey,
Energy evaporated, terror encapsulated,
As threaded and spun, its life force done.

He crept to his kill, now perfectly still,
Palps prepared, and using great skill,
Pulped prey now beaten, the food parcel eaten.
A life force gone. The pattern goes on.

Abduction

Emerging from the coolness of the lush, tropical-green forest, momentarily, the bright sunlight blinded us. And, as we gazed out across the shimmering, smooth and familiar waters which bordered our vast Ashanti tribal homeland, our spirits soared. To-day, we sensed, would be a successful fishing day, enabling us to bring back enough fish for our entire village and, in so doing, earn the respect of our wise chief. Whilst untying, then dragging our old wooden fishing boat from beneath the shade of the gnarled and leafy old baobab, down to the ocean's edge, we recalled the happy wedding celebrations of the previous evening. How, in our ceremonial regalia, stomachs full with rich spicy dishes served on succulent papaya leaves, washed down with plenty of fiery potent brew, we had danced around the giant crackling village fire, its mighty flames licking the air greedily. Later, with our children dozing in its warming glow, we told ancient stories passed down through the generations, whilst expansive navy-blue skies overhead exploded into thousands of shining stars, and the huge milky white moon sat regal and motionless amongst them. It is these traditional tales of our Ashanti ancestors' deeds which help to guide us through our time in this beautiful, bountiful land. It was very late when we fell asleep in our family huts on our colourful woven mats, with our women in our arms, and a cool breeze breathing gently across our decorated breasts. Our sleep was deep and our dreams were sweet but little did we know what dreadful changes were imminent: changes which would alter our lives forever.

As we threw our spears and nets into the bottom of our battered fishing vessel and climbed on board, we began singing our song to the god of the sea, requesting his blessing. We asked that He return us safely to our families. We assured him, just as we always did, that we would take from him only that which was required to feed our tribe. Then singing as we paddled, we left the familiar shore-line with its rich dense forest in the background, our eyes already scouring the clear blue-green ocean waters for shoals of fish, little realising the dangers awaiting us.

A crew of five, sufficient for the canoe to carry, we took turns to dive, spear, let nets out, and haul in, each bounteous catch. All the while observing any dangers, such as changes in the unpredictable ocean waters where the current and the wind might whip up in an instant, as it so often did. For some time we'd been hearing worrying stories about another danger, one we had not yet encountered and hopefully never would. Stories of harsh, white-faced warrior people, dressed in odd-looking clothing, arriving in huge ships laden with powerful weapons. They were said to land unannounced on shores, grab people, then take them by force far across the ocean to unfamiliar lands from which they never returned. We were not sure as to the truth of these stories, though, on occasion, neighbouring tribes beat their warning drums, telling of such dangers. But we, the Ashanti, are a brave, noble and strong warrior people. Under our first beloved chief, Osei Tutu, we fought many victorious battles and were feared by all other tribes. Now, there is rarely a need to fight. Instead, we live in harmony with our neighbours, hunting and tending our own fertile lands, with sufficient game in the forests and fish in the ocean to feed all our people. Our reputation is such that if we had to defend ourselves against new enemies, we would still have more than enough strength to do so.

With the sun now at its hottest our crew, with many successful dives and a full boatload of fish, decided that we should rest a while before returning home. We would eat our bread and share our small cloth bags of food, prepared for us by our loving wives. After eating and resting, the horizon seemed to beckon us once more on to its magical glittering carpet. But we'd completed our task, and so resisted the temptation to continue fishing. Small, almost invisible annoying flies hovered in the air above us, attracted by the odour of the fresh kill around our feet. So, having finished our meal we moved slowly along the familiar coastline, nearer to our home shore-line. But, as we rounded a bend, we were shocked to see a huge, ornately carved and white-sailed wooden ship. It had high sides and tall towering masts. Colourful flags were borne regally aloft, fluttering when caught by a sudden breeze. The ship was anchored just a short way ahead of us, out in the bay, nearer to our disembarking point.

Our hearts beat like a hundred ceremonial battle shields as we wondered what we should do, for we realised immediately that this was the foreboding ship belonging to the fearsome enemy about whom we had been hearing so much. Our first reaction was to seek cover and to observe quietly whilst we decided upon a plan. As a crew of five with little in the way of defensive weapons, and still some way from our village, we wondered how we could hope to defend ourselves let alone consider an attack in broad daylight. We decided that we should continue to stay out of sight and, under cover of darkness, return to our village to report what we'd seen to our chief. He would know what plan of action we warriors should adopt.

It was not long before we heard long and loud mournful cries. They were awful sounds, full of pain and anguish. As we strained our necks and ears, we caught sight of the source. Emerging from the shaded forest in to the light, we saw a long line of people, our people, men women and children, all shackled together in heavy wrist-and-ankle irons, and chains. Our chief was not amongst them, nor any of the more senior members of our village. It was then that we feared that they may already have been killed! Our people were being forced along the beach toward a smaller transportation ship, which would in turn be used to ferry them the short distance to the larger anchored, mother ship. It was as though time had stood still, for we neither spoke nor uttered any sound as we gazed in disbelief at the horrific sight before us. How could this happen to our people - we the strong and mighty Ashanti? The white monsters shouted out in cold rough voices, and lashed out mercilessly at any stragglers or resisters. Many of our people, with blood across their faces and bodies, their clothes ripped and soiled, tried bravely to protect the injured, the women and terrified children, against this ruthless enemy band of six or seven men. Each carried a long heavy looking sword, hanging from a thick leather belt slung casually around the hips; together with a musket, hung loosely beneath the armpit. In their hands they each held lengths of bloodied and knotted rope-lashes, which they used mercilessly to instil fear and order into their prisoners.

As we looked in to one another's sad eyes, we knew we could not stand by meekly and allow these beasts, from who-knows-where, to steal away our families - our people. However daunting the situation appeared, we were the sole members of our tribe who could offer help. Whilst fatigued, we knew we must act swiftly, before our people were herded on board the transporter. Hastily, we formulated a plan. We decided to charge the enemy as they were engrossed in the ferry-boarding operation. The fine sand would dampen any approaching sounds we might make, enabling us a chance to overwhelm them with our only weapons, our tribal spears. Not much when pitted against their weaponry, but we had to try.

Like the stealthy lion, we crept silently out of our boat on to the hot dry sand. Spears in hand, we crouched low behind a rock and awaited our chance. Then, gazelle-like, we leapt lightly across the sand, trying to judge when best to hurl each spear. A single opportunity was all each of us had. Our timing, like our aim, was crucial. The first spear hit its target perfectly. The second also.

Two men felled before they were aware of our presence. As they watched, our people stood paralysed with fear, in disbelief, just like frightened deer on our hunting trips when caught unaware whilst feeding. However, the remaining five foes turned and swung in to action, shouting furiously in their mother-tongue. Now evenly matched, we needed to overwhelm them before they fired their muskets, realising that any shots would alert others of their kind on board their mother ship. As he hurtled toward us, a third lucky spear landed in the chest of the closest of the enemy, bringing him swiftly to his knees before letting out one blood-curdling roar, and then falling backward silently, his fresh brilliant red blood spilled on to the soft yellow sand, disappearing as it became absorbed. Now, whilst larger in fighting numbers, we were under-armed severely and knew we would need to engage in hand-to-hand combat to have any chance of victory. Our final two spears missed their targets, so this was it! Encouraged by the cries of our captive tribal members, now sensing the possibility of freedom, we lunged hot, heavy-footed and wearily at the enemy, trying to find new reserves of energy so badly needed. But these were formidable fighters, not softened as we were by years of peaceful co-existence. They were used to more recent bloody conquests. One of our crew downed one of the devils and, having secured him in a neck lock, snapped it instantly! Another roar went up from our people, which spurred us on. But our successes were brought swiftly to an end when, almost instantly, we were surrounded by a fresh fighting force from the mother ship.

With muskets firing all around us, we were cowed into submission, and the wailing from our people erupted once more. We felt shamed and humiliated by the enemy's swift and sudden advantage. Soon, we too were shackled and whipped into line with our compatriots, then dragged on board the transporter and ferried to the huge, alien-looking mother ship. Once on board, together we were thrown savagely into the foul-smelling pit of the hold, still unaware of the fate which awaited us. Some hours out at sea, the hold was opened. Gasping for air and water, we looked up and pleaded for them to leave it open so that we might be able to breathe. Our plaintive pleas were ignored. Instead, a large cask of water was thrown over us, and the cover of the hold returned us to darkness. In the cramped and foetid darkness lay the whimpering injured, and the terrified children who could not make sense of their circumstances. Drawing closer to loved ones, each tried tragically to gain some comfort, however small. As we lay huddled in this odious prison, scared and vulnerable, we knew that we would never again see our beloved Ashanti homeland or our tribes people. And we despaired.

What is Yellow?

Yellow is the golden sun
Bringing life to everyone.

Yellow the trumpet daffodil
Heralding Spring post Winter's chill.

Yellow the golden timeless sand
Trickling through a playful hand.

Yellow the mellow ripened corn
Rich and ready on an Autumn morn.

Yellow the butter thickly spread
On breakfast toast and fresh warm bread.

Yellow the old man's wrinkled skin
Tired, worn and papery thin.

Yellow the letter he left behind
For the woman he'd loved, and for whom he'd pined.

Yellow and aged, yellow and wan
Pages of a life already done.

The Lost Boy

Winter in eighteenth century Amsterdam, with its grey foreboding skies and its cruel biting winds sweeping across a flat, bleak and colourless landscape: the sheer monotony of it sapping body, mind and soul. But seven-year-old Jan is unusually excited, believing that today will be unlike any other he's experienced so far in his young life. Jan's papa however, feels joyless. Seven days a week, month on month, year on year, as the sole bread-winner of the family, he must trudge wearily to work across the vast network of bridges which span the polluted canal arteries of the busy city. To do otherwise would mean no warming fire for his family, nor food to fill their hollow hungry bellies.

A dyer by trade, he toils endlessly on the canal-side in an exhausting, hot and humid, hole-in-the wall workshop. Each day is spent forcing heavy bolts of fabrics into vast boiling vats of foul smelling liquid. To each, he must add toxic, powdered dyes. Their overwhelming foetid stench irritates eyes and skin. When inhaled, steamy fumes trigger a hacking cough and breathless wheezing fits. Endless prodding, lifting and turning of these heavy loads, in order to obtain an overall colour shade for each vat-full, proves both physically and mentally exhausting. Afterwards, he must haul the fabrics from each into separate containers, trying hard to scald neither himself nor any nearby worker. Many a tired or careless worker has done just that and, as a consequence, has suffered permanent disfigurement or died a slow and agonising death. The long hours of intense physical work mean constant fatigue, an aching back and bones, and an overwhelming dread of illness. On arrival home, saying little, he eats whatever meagre food is available, then falls fast asleep in his chair beside the small hearth in the cramped family living space, until his wife can persuade him to bed down in the adjoining room. Each day the same, with no prospect of change.

Besides Jan, Ma has his young sister, Betsy, to care for. Betsy, just a few weeks old, is puny but with an insatiable appetite. After feeding, little Betsy sucks frantically at her tiny shrivelled clenched fist, wailing and whimpering until, exhausted, she falls asleep. But never for long, causing great anxiety, for the family has lost two children already. One still-born, and the second, almost four years earlier, carried off by the sickness which swept like a demented demon throughout the entire city, taking many with it. Ma frets silently that should another sickness strike Betsy might be taken the same way. As young as he is, Jan is aware that his muteness and deafness, with which he was born, present additional concerns for his anxious mother. Jan tries to minimise these by staying close, knowing how fearful she becomes if he's out of sight for a single moment. The bustling street outside poses considerable dangers. For example, the countless heavily laden unstable carts, and other large loads, pulled daily in all directions along the busy, noisy and narrow canal-side thoroughfares, any of which could mow Jan down in an instant. Then there are the deep, equally traffic-laden polluted canals, with their throngs of trading boats arriving from many distant lands each stacked precariously with their vast cargoes. Ma worries that should Jan wander and get lost, his inability to communicate effectively, together with his wariness of strangers, make him especially vulnerable to danger, so playing outside is out of the question. Jan understands Ma's concerns and tries hard not to complain. But lacking the company of peers makes him feel terribly sad, lonely and isolated. As Betsy grows, Jan hopes maybe life might present greater opportunities for him. But, meanwhile, he understands he just has to be patient.

Due to the extreme weather conditions, the canals quickly freeze over, so become non-operational. The slippery, glassy-surfaced canal-side routes prove especially hazardous. The entire landscape, now clothed in a thick greeny-grey ghostly glow, brings work-places to a standstill and the day is proclaimed a public holiday. News spreads quickly across the city like whispers in the wind. The townspeople decide to gather together on the canals' frozen surfaces, to engage in a rare opportunity for some fun and merriment. Many activities and colourful stalls are erected hastily on the ice. The majority of people, clothed merely in tattered layered rags, rush hurriedly and excitedly to join in. When unexpectedly Pa arrives home, Ma, alarmed, fears he's lost his job, or is maybe ill. But when he explains, Jan beams excitedly, and thinks, "I knew it ... I knew it!"

Arriving at the canal a lively scene meets their eyes. Small groups are huddled around the warmer areas, where flimsily erected stalls sell sweet-smelling roasted savoury treats, and other hot delicacies. Some children, with red-raw hands, hold colourful sticky sweet objects on sticks, trying not to drop them onto the iron-like canal surface. Jan's small nostrils, overwhelmed by the tempting inviting aromas, quiver in anticipation, causing his empty belly to rumble and to roar like a mighty dragon. With great caution, growing throngs move excitedly around. Adults and children of all ages skate and slide on the slippery glassy ice, letting out shrieks of excitement, or fear lest they should end up flat on their backs. Jan's Pa, finding a rough piece of drift-wood, sets to whittling it hastily into a rough boat-like shape, before handing it to a delighted Jan, who instantly trials it on the smooth slippery surface. His heart swells with joy – he has never had such a wonderful toy – and he is especially proud when a small group of boys, some a little older than he, hover nearby gazing wistfully as Jan whizzes the boat along smoothly and gracefully. Jan's parents look on indulgently, happy to witness his relaxed manner in the other boys' company. Soon, all are laughing and playing together, unconcerned by Jan's inability to speak or to hear them. The boat zooms along, speeding from one child to the next. When it misses and sails through skinny, poorly clad legs, with knees and knuckles red and raw, each lets out peals of laughter. When some leave, frozen to the core, others quickly replace them. Jan is elated, having only ever wished for friends to play with. But slowly, the crowds, governed by the cold and other demands, begin dispersing. Ma signals likewise. But when Jan shows such dismay, she relents and conveys that she's taking little Betsy home, but that he and Pa can remain for just a short while longer. Pa nods in agreement, for although perished and exhausted, he understands that for Jan, happy play opportunities are preciously few. The boys continue their games. But minute by minute Jan's Pa's eyelids become heavier, and heavier, as he rests uncomfortably on an abandoned wooden crate.

When next he opens his eyes he feels stiff and completely disoriented. The extreme cold, having engulfed his vulnerable static frame, is now dusted in a covering of light frost. Even his hands, and fingers wrapped carefully in strips of old worn cloth, prove unresponsive to movement and ache badly. He notes the thicker looming skies, now a menacing shroud, making the once poorly visible landscape almost completely invisible. He hears no sound, human nor otherwise, only a deathly hushed silence all around. He panics, knowing that calling out for Jan will prove useless. But it is his only hope – perhaps someone will hear and help. "Jan, Jan my son, where are you? Oh, where are you?" But of course, there is no reply. Gathering himself together he moves slowly, and blindly, this way and that with arms and fingers outstretched, sometimes bumping into abandoned obstacles. And all the while, slipping and sliding, his heart banging wildly in his weak, frail, damaged chest, shouting wildly, "How could I have been so ... so stupid, nodding off like that!" All kinds of potential dangers race through his terrified brain. Trying to keep calm, he attempts to banish his welling tears and calls out more loudly, "Is there no-one around who can help me to find my son?' But the furious, biting winds merely dampen and smother his doleful words.

Suddenly, without warning, he hears a series of low, dull banging sounds, each followed by a short pause. Straining his ears in their direction, Pa inches slowly and carefully toward them. A little louder now, more constant, and desperate, he believes he is nearing their source. With eyes better adjusted to the weather conditions, pa feels certain that he can just make out the small-framed, pathetic, shivering outline of his son, there on the hard ice ahead of him - banging his precious boat as hard as his freezing hands can manage, onto the unforgiving ice in an attempt to attract attention.

"Thank heavens, thank heavens," Pa cries, sweeping his arms around his distraught looking son. "I'm so ... so sorry Jan! I fell asleep. I didn't mean to! Never again, my son! I promise you, never again!"

Bits of the boat debris are strewn visibly about the distressed Jan, now shaking uncontrollably. But having spotted his Pa, nothing else matters. His Pa has found him at last.
Lifting Jan gently up off the cruel glassy surface and hugging his young son tightly, he wraps his worn and tattered coat about him, then begins rubbing Jan's back gently and reassuringly kissing his eyes and face, now awash with hot, steamy tears. Jan couldn't explain how he and the boys, so engrossin in their fun, had moved so far from their initial playing area. One-by-one the group

dwindled, leaving Jan to continue playing independently. He'd been so happy. But now he was at his happiest. Initially, when he'd looked about him and noticed so few people around, he'd tried hard to find his Pa, but that had proved useless. It was then that Jan had decided to stay put and to wait for his pa to find him. He'd realised that by moving constantly he might distance himself still further from his Pa.

Jan's Pa, despite his fatigue, continued carrying Jan all the way off the frozen canal, hugging him close, fearful that should he let him go his treasured son might somehow disappear forever. Nestled into his Pa's chest, Jan knew just how much he was loved, and that now he was completely safe. That night as Jan cuddled up close beside his family in their confined sleeping space, he felt that he was the most fortunate child in all Amsterdam. And, despite some of the day's fraught events, it *had* been the happiest day of his life, and one he would never, ever, forget.

Jude Painter

When Jude begins to read, we always know that something unexpected will happen – and that often, she will make us laugh. Ed.

Sometimes I get a clear, detailed visual image of what I want to write about; at others, the odd word or phrase will set me off.

I think it is amazing what is inside of us all, and how we can set it free by just beginning to write.

Hot June

Brian was sitting in the sun under the apple tree lost in a thriller. When he read a good book he became entirely immersed in the story often being totally transported from his own, some would say rather dull life, to the world he was reading about. So that it was some time before he was aware that Gloria was speaking to him. "I really think that you and I should go over to Michael and Samantha's place to do some work in the house and garden this afternoon," she said.

"Why should we?" demanded Brian. "We have things to do in our own house, and I'm only too glad to have a bit of peace and enjoy being on our own for once."

"We'll be on our own over at their place – they won't be there doing any work this weekend. They're off to Glastonbury."

"You mean to tell me they'll be having the time of their lives at Pilton and we'll be slaving away in their house and garden?" He rose indignantly, throwing his hat into the shrubbery then standing, hands on hips, in a familiar attitude of outrage.

"Yes, I know darling, it doesn't seem quite fair," Gloria replied calmly. "But look at it this way; the sooner the renovations on their house are completed, the sooner they'll be able to move out of ours."

The young couple had moved in with the Blisses shortly after they left university. Samantha's parents were wealthy and had an impressive six bed-roomed house with a swimming pool, so

Michael's parents had been surprised that the young couple had chosen to move into their own modest, three bed-roomed semi. When Gloria made the tentative suggestion that the couple might be more comfortable in her parents' home, Sam replied airily "Oh, Mummy and Daddy couldn't possibly have us to live with them – she's terribly bothered by her nerves."

Shortly after Sam, whom they had not met many times previously, and their son, had moved into Chestnut Avenue, Gloria and Brian were happily watching University Challenge in the sitting room when they were assailed by the most shocking burst of girlish laughter from Michael's room. It was hard to describe the sound but it began like a sort of neighing, increasing in volume until it became an odd intermittent donkey-like braying. Neither of them had ever heard anything like it before. Gloria rolled her eyes upwards. "So now we know why Mummy has bad nerves and can't have Samantha to live with her!"

In spite of the 'equine laugh' as Brian called it, which still, after four months had the power to make Brian and Gloria break glasses and drop things, the four got on surprisingly well.

The whole country was enjoying a mini heat-wave, and there was the smell of freshly mown hay in the Somerset air. The grass verges were full of moon daisies, buttercups and wild poppies, and swifts swooped out of the clear blue skies for insects as Brian and Gloria drove to the cottage. All over the country the record-breaking hot weather was causing people to plaster themselves with factor thirty sun cream and write to the papers. Others were rushing to the crowded beaches, resulting in huge traffic jams.

Gloria set to work to strip the paintwork in the interior of the nearly derelict cottage which Sam's father had helped the young couple to buy at auction, while Brian with his secateurs and his new scythe set off into the large bramble-strewn, weed-choked wilderness which would one day become the garden and orchard. At the last moment Gloria called him back to warn him to watch out for adders basking on the path.

Brian could not even find a path but he did start to think about snakes. Before he had cut and slashed his way though twenty feet he was sweating profusely and bothered by horseflies and mosquitoes. The undergrowth had not been touched for years, so much of it was head-height. Brian suddenly felt very alone.

He realised that the territory he was now in was hostile in the extreme. Not only were there stinging, biting insects, but also pit vipers and deadly coral snakes. Furthermore the area was the home of several rival drug cartels who ran makeshift laboratories amongst the trees to process and package cocaine and its derivatives. His task was to explore the region and report back to a handler in Tumaco and then to London. Using his excellent Spanish he was to try if possible to locate and recruit any villagers who would be willing to pass information on about the local drug lords. He also had to try to sow distrust between the different narcos.

He knew it was a dangerous mission and that three or maybe four other agents of 'the firm' had disappeared in this part of the world; the only evidence of the last one's capture and subsequent torture had been the grizzly severed ear sent by special delivery to the Whitehall office.

Brian recalled the day some months before when B.K. had called him into the office and outlined the job to him. "Look, Bliss old chap, I'll be honest with you. The UK is awash with these foul drugs. We have decided to tackle the problem at source and you are the man for the job, perhaps the only man. We've lost too many good chaps already and there are departmental cuts. Brexit is also a problem for us, need I go on?" He continued, "I know you have done seven successful missions in the past year and have surely earned a bit of R and R but I am going to beg you to take on just one more." He looked intently into Brian's face, the nervous tick in his left eye betraying his anxiety lest Brian refuse.

"Actually B.K. it was eight missions. Are you forgetting Tunbridge Wells?"

"Oh! God no, eight missions. I could never forget Tunbridge Wells!" He continued, "This time it will be different, you will be acting totally alone. You will have no radio contact and be armed only with such weapons as you can carry in a small hold-all. If you are caught HMG will deny all knowledge, you know... the usual."

Brian considered for a split second. He thought of poor Gloria alone at home once again, week after week not knowing where he was or if he would ever return. Quickly he reached his decision, stood to attention and saluted, "Sir, I will do it. I'll do it for Frobisher," he said with a catch in his throat, "because of the promise I made to him that day.

Suddenly the sound of a helicopter approaching rapidly from the west brought him back to the present, interrupting his thoughts. It could be the police, many of whom were in the pay of the drug cartels, or it might be Martinez's own vehicle. With the sort of money he made from his narcotics business he and the other narcos could buy anyone or anything they wanted. Yes, the helicopter was a brand new XC1002 Russian-made, Brian could tell from the note of the engine. He flattened himself onto the filthy soil and rolled as far under the thorny branches as he could, lacerating himself as he did so, ignoring the fact that most of his wounds would probably become seriously infected.

The helicopter flew off towards the north and Brian allowed himself a brief sigh of relief. Then with horror he watched it circle and return, zig-zagging across the sky above him, searching the ground below. He wondered who had betrayed him. Could it be the barman he had suspected of spiking his drink the previous night, or the glamorous blonde who had paid him so much unexpected attention? He had no time to speculate. It was now vital he get to the shelter of the trees as fast as he could. It seemed to him as if crawling under the cover of the lowest plants might be the only way to cover the vast distance and be unseen from the air, but the ground was becoming boggy and he knew the giant anacondas could be a problem.

Crawling on his hands and knees his progress was painfully slow. Looking to the right he noticed a procession of killer ants moving purposefully towards him, forcing him to elevate to a crouching shuffle. Once, three years before, he had seen what remained of the body of a man who had been trapped in river mud after the soldier ants had finished with him. It was a sight he would never forget.

The helicopter seemed to have flown away and Brian moved tentatively towards the trees, hacking at the vines and thorny branches which barred every step of his way. He heard the bark of a dog followed by a chilling chorus of howling. It sounded as if they were large angry dogs. Brian still had a vestigial fear of big dogs ever since a holiday at Pately Bridge just after his fourth birthday.

The helicopter pilot must have alerted the narcos and their heavies on the ground, who would now be scouring the jungle for him. His blood froze. A moment later he made one of the lightening quick decisions he was trained to make, his mind functioning like an advanced computer.

He plunged into the nearby river, knowing that the dogs would not be able to scent him in water. By this time he was seriously exhausted, in spite of the twenty mile runs and hour of circuit training he did most week days. The heavy JPT 16 with the 30+ magazine in his pocket was impeding his progress.

He was just wondering whether to jettison the gun or the

machete, either of which he would have to carry between his teeth to leave his hands free for swimming, when he heard a soft purring like a distant motor boat engine. He turned and saw a custard-coloured cat sitting on a nearby rock in the sunshine staring at him in a knowing way... and then he heard Gloria calling.

Journey

The days are so hot and dusty; the heat makes the desert shimmer and the wind causes the sand to sting our eyes. We plod day after day across the rocky scrub with eagles soaring ever watchful above us. Our little party must look like a procession of tiny ants as we trudge so slowly across this huge desert.

On the third day we are climbing a mountain and I suddenly notice his foot above me on the track, dust-covered with cracked skin around the heel. It is the foot of a stranger, totally unfamiliar. My feelings overwhelm me as I realise how little I know this tall, quiet man. My husband seems so different from my brother or any of the young men in my village who I might have expected to marry. He speaks hardly at all and to me he seems as strange and foreign as the land we are passing through.

The journey has now settled into a routine. My husband wakes me early each morning while it is still dark and cool. We eat a handful of dates and drink a little water or wine and begin our walk through the day. At about midday when the sun is at its very hottest and I feel so exhausted I believe I cannot take another step we find some small cave or a little pile of rocks where we can sleep out of the sun for a couple of hours. Then we resume our journey.

At night we make a little fire which helps to keep the curious jackals away, although we can still hear them howling and scratching in the undergrowth. At first the sounds of the animals invisible all around us frightened me but now that they have become more familiar to me and my husband is close by I find I like listening to them, thinking of these creatures all going about their affairs in the dark.

He lies near me but does not share my blanket. When I ask him why, he says that he will come to me afterwards. He does not touch me, although when the donkey stumbled yesterday, he was nearby and quick to reach out his hand to stop me from falling.

We have two donkeys; one is for me to ride when I am tired or when my back aches and the other to carry our goods, the cooking pan, some food and blankets. He has a big load because we do not know when or even if we will return home.

The younger donkey was frightened yesterday by a snake on the mountain path and stood petrified, unwilling to move a single step. My father would have sworn and beaten it but my husband showed no anger, stroking the animal's muzzle and speaking softly in her ear. I was surprised and did not think this gentle way would work, but though still clearly terrified she leaned into him and slowly walked on.

Sometimes I am uncomfortable and the baby kicks so I cannot sleep. Then I begin to be afraid for the future, that I will not be a worthy mother, that this thing that is happening is too big for me, that I am not ready. Last night I saw by his eyes glittering in the moonlight that he was also awake. Maybe he was thinking similar thoughts, worrying about whether he has done the right thing in marrying a young girl he hardly knows; a girl who is carrying a child which is not his own, wondering if we will grow to love one another – wondering how it will all end.

Lost

She did not give any thought to what she was doing. After she had seen them her instinct was to just grab her bag and coat and flee the party. There was nobody to say goodbye to, nobody who was even aware that she had left: nearly everyone in the house was a stranger to her. They were all Pete's friends and colleagues.

She had not wanted to come. The guests would all be people from Pete's work and she was sure she would not know anyone, but he had persuaded her. *So that's why you were so keen to come,* she muttered to herself through clenched teeth. *Because she was going to be there, so available and so willing, so bloody willing.*

Bridie strode down the wet path thrusting her arms into her coat sleeves. *Why did you bring me, you bastard, if you just wanted to go off with that bitch?* she railed to herself, buttoning her coat and pulling the belt tight. She turned right onto the main road, thinking of nothing but her fury and humiliation, knowing that anger was the emotion that was keeping her going; that if for one moment she stopped seething she might weep.

So Bridie walked fast, heedless of the rain, holding onto her dignity. She decided that she would ring for a taxi, except that she did not know where she was and remembered that her phone was in Pete's car still plugged into the charger. *Anyway if I keep walking I'm sure to find a taxi rank or office. Then I'll get back to the flat and trash his CD collection, tear up his precious football magazines, write profanities on his walls, tell him just what I think of the bastard.* She remembered hearing about a wronged woman, *another poor bloody cow*, she thought bitterly, who had hidden prawns in her former lover's hollow curtain track. He had gone nearly mad trying to locate the source of the increasingly terrible smell over the following weeks. She gave a grim little laugh. As she marched on, her feelings swung between wanting to never see Pete again to wanting to kill him or demand he tell her just what it about Tracey that made her so attractive to him; what did that girl have that she didn't have? Some instinct of self-protection told her that she should not go there, that now was not a good time to start speculating about her own possible deficiencies.

She realised that she must have walked farther than shed meant to because the neatly gardened houses of suburbia where the party had been held had given way to streets lined with unlit depressed looking charity shops and dark shuttered lock-ups and she had not the least idea where she was. Soggy fast food containers littered the pavements and there were puddles between the cracked paving slabs. Torn posters flapped wetly from the lamp posts.

She wondered whether she should turn back and try to retrace her steps but decided she had probably come too far. Just then she saw a welcome patch of bright light ahead and quickened her steps, hoping it was a late-opening take away or somewhere public where she could at least find out which part of town she was in and phone for a taxi. By now the rain was falling steadily and she was feeling soaked and uncomfortable.

As she drew close Bridie saw that it was a nightclub with a whole group of young men milling around outside. They seemed to be having some sort of an argument with two bouncers in black. It looked as if the youths were drunk and the bouncers were refusing to let them in. She crossed the road and hurried on, head down. One of the youths shouted out to her and said something to the other men who laughed. They turned to stare at her and she felt a moment's fear that they would turn their attention to her. There was the sound of a bottle smashing which distracted them and she increased her pace.

She continued walking for some time, increasingly aware that her expensive shoes were giving her blisters and probably disintegrating. She thought it strange that there were no other pedestrians about, though she could hear footsteps somewhere behind her. She realised that it must be a great deal later than she had supposed. A car approached her with its windows open and swerved through a large gritty puddle alongside the kerb, sending a sudden shock of icy water over her, soaking her legs and splashing up her body. She heard the occupants of the car calling and laughing as it accelerated away. She felt her eyes begin to fill with tears.

She thought then that as well as having just been betrayed by her boyfriend she was miserable, lost, wet through and frightened. Her situation seemed impossibly bad but she knew she should try to be strong, to hold the panic at bay for as long as she could. *Surely I'll meet someone soon who'll help me or just tell me where I am. Where is everyone? Surely I'll reach a residential area before long where I can knock on a door... or a taxi will come,* she muttered, attempting to reassure herself. She limped resolutely on past an abandoned builders' yard towards a dark churchyard, the footsteps keeping a steady pace behind her.

Antique Market

Dad had wandered off somewhere, chatting to other stall-holders – especially Nell on antique linens, I suspected. I was going to dust the stock a bit but then got distracted by reading the report on the Taunton first team's match the previous Saturday.

So I didn't notice the man's approach until he was standing right over me. He gave a polite cough.

"Last time I was here I noticed that you – and your father, I presume it is – keep some rather unusual items. So I thought you might be interested to see what I have here. I would like to venture that you have never beheld anything like it before," he said with a smile he probably hoped was mysterious. In the short time I have been working with Dad, I've seen so many elderly people present us with some awful piece of damaged tat that they wanted us to buy that I didn't have much hope, although in this business there is always the chance that you might find something special.

As he reached into the large M&S carrier bag he was holding, I took the opportunity to have a good look at him. I saw that he was very old with a small neatly trimmed iron grey beard, contrasting oddly with his white longish hair. He also had dark eyebrows bushing above his glasses and two or three clearly visible long hairs emerging from his nostrils.

He was unsteady on his feet so I brought him a chair and invited him to open his bag. "Thank you, young man...so kind. I'm not as steady on my feet as I used to be."

He spoke with a slight Eastern European accent, hardly noticeable at all, as if he had lived in England for a long time. He gave the impression of being one of those cultured and excessively courteous elderly gentlemen who you don't meet often these days.

"The rare object I have to offer you has been in my family for generations and is, I believe, valuable as well as being extremely powerful." As he spoke he began to fiddle with the knots in the string around his treasure. In a slow painstaking way he undid each one and coiled every piece of string carefully before placing it in his pocket. He then began removing sheet after sheet of the newspaper it was wrapped in. This was old and yellowing and the words I could see had Cyrillic lettering. This made the parcel somehow more mystifying and I found I was becoming increasingly interested. He smoothed and laid each sheet on the floor beside him.

At last he pulled out a spherical parcel and then like a conjuror he removed the final wrapping with a flourish to reveal a thin, glass, silvered ball about the size of a small football. It resembled a large Christmas tree bauble with a ring at the top by which it could be suspended. I noticed it looked very old, with some of the silvering speckled and damaged. I had never seen anything like it before.

"This is known as a witch's ball. My great-grandparents first owned it. They were little more than peasants really, in actuality I am the first educated man in my family," he said tossing his head and smoothing the hair at his temple. "They hung this in their front window for the whole of their lives. In time, it was passed down to my father and he and my mother did the same. They always kept the ball hanging in the window in full view of the street. Mutti would never take it down, not even when she was cleaning the glass. The belief was that any witch seeking to enter the house would see her reflection and be so horrified and frightened by it that she would go away and leave the household in peace".

"That is fascinating!" I said sincerely, smiling and reaching out to take it, forgetting not to reveal how much I was beginning to want this curiosity.

"When I inherited the witch ball I was rather an arrogant young man and being educated I dismissed such things as mere peasant superstition. Nothing would have persuaded me to hang such an object in my window, so I left it wrapped in the attic with other heirlooms I had no use for. I went off to university and met the lady I later married. Recently I have decided to dispose of it. Now it is too late for me," he said sadly, staring into the distance, "but it may help somebody else."

"It is a fascinating story. However, the object is not in very good condition," I remembered to say, and then to pause, and casually ask: "How much would you want for it?"

"Oh, I could not possibly sell it. It would be very unlucky to sell a witch's ball. What I propose is that you buy this other article from me for what you would have paid for it and I include the witch's ball as a gift."

By now I was becoming keen to own the object, and hoping not to reveal the interest by my expression, I pretended to carefully examine the crudely carved wooden stag lounging against a pine tree which he handed me.

"I will leave you to consider while I check in with home – my wife always likes to know where I am." He took out his mobile phone. "Hello, my dear, it's me." He paused and listened. "Oh, I was hoping to take a little time in the Vivary Park enjoying the spring flowers, but if you want me to come straight home I will forgo my little treat." He rang off and looked at me. "My wife is a...well let's just say, a demanding lady. Now, I can see you are ready to purchase the antique rustic carving and of course have the witch's ball as my gift to you," he continued, rubbing his hands together.

We haggled for a while but my heart was not in it. I was fascinated by the old man and the story of the witch's ball and had such a strong compulsion to own it that I hardly thought about the cost. This was one object which I would not be adding to our stock.

As we concluded our business and I handed him the cash, he gripped my hand tightly. "I urge you not to allow your education, and a young man's contempt for those ancient things you do not understand, to lead you to underestimate the power of this witch's ball."

Glancing at the object for one last time he fixed me with those sad blue eyes for a long moment before staring pointedly at the mobile phone still in his hand.

Then he left, without another word.

Rainy Saturday

As she came out of the warmth of Tesco, Gloria felt the cold rain lash against her face. A sudden gust of wind caught a plastic carrier bag and slapped it wetly against her leg.

She swore, peeled the object off and stuffed it into the corner of her trolley which she manoeuvred, with difficulty, to her car. It was not until it had been three quarters filled with her shopping that it had revealed itself to be severely disabled with a distinct list to the left. Panting with the effort she unloaded her bags into the back of the Focus and sent the trolley crashing into its fellows cowering in the trolley shelter.

Her two dogs greeted her enthusiastically snuffling amongst the bags. The smell of wet dog was eye-wateringly strong. She had combined driving them to their favourite muddy wood to walk with doing the weekly supermarket trip, thinking it would be a good idea to kill two birds with one stone; an impulse she was regretting as the scent of wet dog hit her. The car was badly steamed up with their hot breath and steaming coats. She had to fumble in her pocket to find a scrap of tissue to wipe all the windows. She thought of Brian relaxing in the warm fug of the pub enjoying the match on Sky TV and for a moment envied him.

He had in fact come out of the Lamb and Flag once but then returned for his umbrella. The public bar was still full of post-match euphoria as the local team had probably, no, almost certainly, gained promotion to the Championship next season.

People began slapping him on the back once more, offering him congratulations and drinks almost as if he had been responsible for the victory.

Laughingly waving these aside Brian turned up his collar and, raising his umbrella against the still pouring rain, he made his way down the street towards Tesco. Coloured lights from the shops were reflected brightly in the puddles and a passing car sent up sparkling beads of spray. People were hurrying but he saw no reason to rush. He stopped to watch a little boy in a red plastic raincoat and yellow sou'wester hat jump with both feet into a large dirty puddle, repeating this several times with an expression of utter joy on his little face before being hustled away by his angry mother.

Brian stepped around the puddle and began humming to himself:- tumty, tump, tump, tumty, tump tump.... His feet took up the rhythm, his steps taking him between and then through the puddles. In his mind's eye he could see the awe and admiration on the child's face.

His joyous singing became louder as he wheeled the umbrella around him, high and low in extravagant circles leaping and cavorting around the scurrying pedestrians. A lamp post stood just ahead, its light pooling on the pavement, reminding him that now might be the perfect time for him to attempt the famous one-armed-around-the-lamppost swing stunt he had almost perfected when he was at college.

He heard the accompanying music rise in a crescendo as

he took off purposefully, still singing, his speed and grace propelling him through the air, his legs and feet flying sideways as he executed the almost perfect movement.

At that moment Gloria's Ford Focus stopped beside the curb and the passenger door swung open. Just as he was retrieving his shoe from the gutter he remembered to glance around for the umbrella – but there was no sign of it…

Sue Purkiss

The seed of a story can be sown long before it is actually written. I was at university in Durham, and I remember hearing the story then of how, during the war, on the night of a German bombing raid, a mist rose up and hid the tower of the cathedral so that the bombers didn't see it and it was saved. It was said that Saint Cuthbert, who is buried in the cathedral, was responsible for the miracle. That was the beginning of *A Pile of Stones*.

The other story has a much more recent origin. I like to write stories prompted by postcards – usually, I write the story on the back of the postcard. (I have very small writing!) For this one, though, I used a photo I'd taken on a recent visit to Elsinore in Denmark, and I didn't confine myself to writing on the back of it.

A Pile of Stones

Megan closed her library book. It was called *The Thirty Nine Steps*. It was by John Buchan, and it was a really thrilling story about a dashing hero called Richard Hannay who almost single-handedly saved England from the enemy. If she was Richard Hannay, she'd know *exactly* how to set about rescuing her dad from his prison camp in Germany. She sighed.

"I was in the butcher's this morning," Mrs Keithley from next door was saying. "They said the Germans bombed York the other night. Ethel Smart said they only missed the Minster by a whisker – can you credit that now?"

"It's wicked," said Mam with a frown. "Bombing a beautiful church like that. They should be ashamed of themselves, the heathens."

Mrs Keithley nodded. "They do say," she went on, lowering her voice and looking, Megan thought, quite excited, "that they're going to bomb *all* the cathedrals. They do say that it might he *Durham* next!"

Mam's face went chalk white. "No! They can't do that! Why – if they bombed the cathedral, our Ted would have nothing to come home to!"

Mrs Keithley looked alarmed. "Oh, there now, pet, it's all right. It's just people talking – nothing in it, I'm sure. Here – I'll just make us another cup of tea, shall I?"

That night, Megan lay awake, staring at the crack in the ceiling. Sometimes she imagined it would split open, and she'd fly out through the gap right across Europe to where Dad was held prisoner. She'd take him his favourite cake – fruit cake with butter on – and a packet of tea in case they didn't have any in prison camps. The butter would be a bit tricky because it was hard to come by these days, but she would save up her ration specially for him. The plan was to bring him back home, but she wasn't sure if she'd be able to fly with a passenger.

But tonight, she was thinking about what Mrs Keithley had said. Before the war, Dad had been a stonemason at the cathedral. Her grandfather had been one too, and his father before him, and his before him. That's what the Campions did, they looked after the cathedral. To Dad, it wasn't just a job, it was his life. Before he'd gone off to war, he'd gone round to all his favourite bits of the great cathedral, laying his hand on the old stones and whispering to them. She knew he'd done this, because he'd taken her with him and she'd watched.

"You're in charge now, Megan," he'd told her solemnly. "You'll have to take care of it till I'm home again." And she'd promised she would.

So it was up to her. It was a promise, and promises were sacred. Somehow, she had to save the cathedral.

The next day was a Thursday. After school, instead of walking home with Wendy and Elaine, she told them she was going to meet her mother in town. Once they were out of sight, she hurried down the steep hill towards the river, planning to climb up the path to the cathedral.

But something was happening. There were firemen unwinding long coils of hosepipe at the bottom of the path, and lots of policemen standing about looking important. She stared. Then she understood. They were going to draw water from the river and take it up to the cathedral. So it was true. They *did* think there was going to be a raid. She had a sudden vision of flames licking at the stones of the beloved building... no, she wouldn't let it happen! She plucked at the sleeve of a policeman who was standing watching the firemen.

"Please mister," she said. "is it true? Are the Germans coming? Are they going to bomb Durham?"

He looked down at her, startled. "What? Now then, wherever did you get that idea? Hurry along there, pet, and don't get in the way."

A much fiercer looking policeman was heading towards her. Megan sidestepped him and ran along the path till she got to Prebends' Bridge. She'd get to the cathedral that way, up the Bailey. She didn't know what she was going to do when she got there, but she was quite certain it was where she had to be.

Usually, it was very peaceful in the cloisters. Dad had often pointed out to her the way the stone slabs had been gently hollowed by centuries and centuries of feet, and she loved to think of that, loved to think of all those generations of monks and stonemasons going about their work, praying and hammering and chiselling. Durham had a castle too, on the other side of Palace Green, but it was nothing compared to the cathedral.

Today, though, everything felt too still. No-one was about. The air was clagged with tension. She hesitated. What about the Bishop? He was the one in charge, wasn't he? Perhaps he was in the cathedral, praying that the Germans would go somewhere else. She hurried on.

Once inside the main body of the cathedral, she looked round. How could anything threaten these massive pillars, these thick stone walls? It had stood for so many centuries – what could a few little planes do to damage it?

But she knew what they could do. She'd seen the pictures in the papers.

She walked slowly towards the shrine of St Cuthbert and the tomb of the Venerable Bede. It was a part of the cathedral she had always liked. It was on a smaller scale than the soaring nave, and she liked the way the way the light slanted in through the windows. The cathedral stood on an outcrop of rock within a loop of the River Wear. If you could climb up a ladder and look out through those windows, you would be able to see down to the river, then up to Crossgate Peth. Her street was further on, up near the viaduct. Sometimes they went on the train to visit Auntie Iris in Darlington, and as it crossed the viaduct on the way back, you got this amazing view of the cathedral, hunched above the city like a great eagle. What would her father feel when he came home if he looked across from the viaduct and saw nothing but a heap of ruins? She blinked away tears. What was she going to *do*?

"Please," she whispered. "*Please* – don't let them bomb the cathedral!"

Then she had a sudden sense that someone was watching her – a kind of tingling on the back of her neck. She turned, and saw a priest. She hadn't noticed him when she came in. Could he have been behind one of the pillars? Though these pillars, unlike the ones in the nave, were slender – surely less than the width of a man. She couldn't see him very clearly; perhaps her eyes were still teary, she thought, and she blinked again, hard. He wore a shabby brown robe, scruffier than the long black cassocks the priests usually wore. The air shifted, as if someone had opened a door somewhere. She heard the shouts of the firemen outside, but they sounded a long way off. She caught a scent of something fresh and tangy; it was like the sea, she thought, and yet the coast was miles away.

Then she looked at his face, and she forgot everything else. She'd never seen such a face. It was old and young, playful and wise, happy and sad, all at the same time. His eyes were like a summer sea, blue-green, calm on the surface but deep, very deep. He smiled at her.

"You are sad," he said. His voice sounded creaky, as if he hadn't used it lately. "Is there something wrong?"

Something *wrong*?

"Yes," she said in a rush. "Of course there is! My Dad got

captured at a place called Dunkirk, and he's a prisoner, and Mam has to work in the factory and there's no sweets any more. And Mrs Keithley says the Germans are going to bomb the cathedral, and I think it might be tonight, because they're laying out a great big long hosepipe and the planes always come at night – and if they bomb the cathedral how will Dad find his way home? And even if he does, he'll be really sad, because he works here, he's a stonemason, and he told me I was to look after it while he was away, but I don't know how to do it!"

And then she burst into tears, really properly this time.

He didn't say anything, but slowly, she began to feel calm. It was light where he stood, she noticed. It must have been the early evening sun through the windows.

"So many wars," he said sadly. "I keep thinking they'll stop, but they never do. And this one is the worst of all, isn't it?"

She nodded. He gestured towards some steps near St Cuthbert's shrine, and they went over and sat down.

"I think the last one was bad too," she said.

"The Great War," he said. "Yes. That was very bad."

She looked at him. He sounded as if he knew what he was talking about. "Were you in it?" she said.

"Oh yes. I've been in every war. For hundreds of years. First they had spears and swords, then it was bows and arrows, then it was guns, and now –"

"Now it's bombs," she said.

She suddenly realised what he had said. She looked at him,

and opened her mouth to speak, but then she noticed something. The light around him wasn't coming from the windows, it was coming from the monk himself. She drew back, startled.

"Who – who are you?" she stammered.

He smiled, and nodded towards the shrine.

She followed his gaze. Then she looked back at him in disbelief. "You don't mean...? You're not – you can't be St Cuthbert! He's been dead for hundreds of years!"

But somehow, though her mind struggled to grasp it, somewhere deep down she knew it was true. And she realised with a thrill of excitement that he was exactly what – or who – she needed. Dad had often told her how the cathedral had been built specially to shelter St Cuthbert's shrine. It was his church, his place, so he was bound to look after it.

"Why then," she gabbled excitedly, "*you* can do it! *You* can save the cathedral!"

He shook his head. "Oh no. I'm sorry, but I can't do that. I'm just a simple monk. I mustn't interfere."

Shocked, she jumped up. "Simple monks don't go walking around and chatting to people hundreds of years after they've died!"

"Fourteen hundred years," he agreed. "Or is it thirteen? You lose track after a bit."

She stamped her foot. "Never mind how long it is! You can do it, of course you can!"

He looked down at his hands. They were very thin, she

noticed. She could almost see through them. "Oh, Megan," he said. "It isn't that simple. It really isn't."

"Then what's the use of being a saint?" she cried, bewildered. "Saints do miracles, don't they? Well, if you won't make one to save your own church, then I won't believe in you! And I won't believe in God either! I won't have anything more to do with *any* of it!"

And she ran away from him, back through the cathedral, through the cloisters, down the Bailey and back to the river. Her heart was full of bitterness, and she didn't look back once.

She was determined to stay awake that night. She would keep watch, she told herself. She knew her job, even if St Cuthbert didn't know his. But she felt so sleepy that she just had to close her eyes… and then she saw Cuthbert again. He was kneeling before an altar in a simple stone church with a thatched roof. It was on a tiny island, and she could hear the sound of the sea. The wind howled like a siren. Then suddenly there were real sirens, screaming from the castle. She jumped up and ran to the window. In the moonlight, the cathedral shone like a beacon. Then she heard a distant hum, a low thrumming drone. It grew steadily louder, till she felt the house begin to shake.

"Oh, no!" she whispered, stricken. The planes were coming, and you could see the cathedral as clear as day. They couldn't possibly miss it.

Then she heard another sound. It was a voice, strong and

powerful, like waves thundering onto the shore – Cuthbert's voice. It grew louder and louder, till it filled the whole sky and drowned the sound of the bombers. Then, as she watched, a thick white mist rose from the river. It drifted up the hill and wrapped itself round the cathedral till there was not a stone to be seen. The cathedral had utterly vanished. Megan stared. It had happened so quickly she could hardly take it in.

The first planes roared overhead. The sound was almost unbearable, but Cuthbert's voice was silent now. Megan took one more disbelieving look at the place where the cathedral had been, and then she ran downstairs and she and Mam hurried into the shelter in Mrs Keithley's garden.

No bombs fell on Durham that night.

In the city next day, no-one talked of anything else. It was a miracle, they said – there was no other explanation. St Cuthbert had protected his own. Megan's eyes shone with pride, and as soon as she could, she hurried back up to the cathedral, hoping and praying he would be there.

He was.

"You did it!" she cried, bursting with gratitude. "You saved the cathedral!"

But why was he so sad? His eyes, when he raised his head and looked at her, were like the sea in winter, grey and grim.

"Do you know what happened in the Derwent Valley?" he said quietly.

She shook her head.

"There's a loop in the river there, very like the one here. And there's a ruined priory, Finchale. And a viaduct. The planes dropped their bombs there. They must have thought it was Durham. Eight people were killed, three of them children."

"Oh no! But – but… people would have been killed here, too," she faltered.

He shrugged. "Perhaps. Who knows?" He sighed, and the sound was like a cold east wind. "I hope your father comes home, Megan. I know he loves the cathedral. But it's only a pile of stones, when all is said and done."

She felt stricken, and he smiled at her gently. "Never mind, child. We did our best."

She reached out and touched the pillar nearest to her, as if it would give her comfort. When she looked back, the cathedral was empty.

A Winter's Night In Helsingør

The winter nights were long in Helsingør, and the wind from the sea whistled down the narrow alley ways. But in the little house with the timbered front and the small-paned windows, the fire on the hearth was warm, and its light flickered on the face of the grandmother as she sat on the old oak settle, made comfortable with cushions stuffed with goose feathers. On one side of her was her grandson, Henrik, and on the other was little Maya. It was the best time of the day for them; they had eaten fried fish and potatoes, and they were feeling warm and full and just a little bit sleepy.

"So," said the grandmother. "You want a story, do you?

Well, let me see what I can do."

"Tell us about a troll!" said Henrik, his eyes shining. "A really fierce and nasty one!"

"Oh, no!" said Maya. "I don't want to have bad dreams."

Grandmother hugged her. "What kind of a story would you like then, my little cherub?"

Maya thought.

"She's silly!" said Henrik, a little sulkily. "See, she can't think of anything."

"Yes I can! Just a minute now... a princess! Tell us a story about a princess!"

Henrik groaned. But the grandmother's face softened, and her eyes turned a little misty.

"Ah!" she said. "Well, I can't think right now of a story about a princess. But I can tell you one about a prince. A real one!"

That was good enough for both of them. They snuggled in close, and the grandmother began her tale.

"It was long, long ago, in this very town. I was just a girl then, and your grandfather and I hadn't been married very long. He was a fisherman, of course, just like your father, with his own boat, earning a good living." She raised her head and listened for a moment. They all heard the wind howling outside, and the rain splattering on the windows. "But you know how bad the storms can be, and how cruel the sea. I came from a farm, and every time your grandfather went out to sea on a bad night, my heart was in my mouth until he came safely home again.

"Well, it was a winter's night, very like this one. I had expected Erik back the day before, and when he didn't come, I was beside myself with worry. I tried to sleep, but all I could hear was the howling of the wind and the hammering of the rain. It never let up, and I couldn't stop thinking of that little boat, tossing about on the waves. In the end, I'd had enough. I got up, wrapped myself in a warm shawl and my thick cloak, and went down to the quayside, flitting through the streets like a ghost. There was a little bit of light from the moon behind the clouds, and one or two windows had candles in them. I remember thinking that everyone should put a candle in their window, and then the town would be a beacon of light to bring Erik safely home.

"When I got down to the harbour, at first it seemed as if there was no-one else there. I could see nothing but the boats at anchor creaking restlessly, as if they wanted to be on the move. They were great ships, some of them, from as far away as England and Russia – just like now, they all have to pass through the sound and pay their dues to the king in his castle.

"But then the moon suddenly broke through the clouds, and I saw a man standing gazing out to sea. He was dressed in a long black cloak and he stood as still as a statue. In fact for a minute, I thought that's what he was, until I saw his hair blowing back from his face in the wind.

"Oh dear, his face! It was so pale – white as chalk. I don't mind admitting, I felt frightened then – I thought perhaps he *was* a ghost – a real one!"

"I'm not sure I like this story," whispered Maya.

"I do!" said Henrik.

Grandmother laughed, and hugged Maya. "It's all right. He wasn't a ghost. He was a young man, and a handsome one too."

"Oh," said Henrik, disappointed.

The rain on the window sounded like fingers tapping, and the grandmother's face went misty again as she remembered that winter's night so long ago.

"He looked sad," she whispered. "So sad. I couldn't bear it. For a moment I stopped thinking about your grandfather and I went across to the man and put my hand on his arm.

"What is it?" I said. "Is there anything I can help you with?"

"I don't think he'd noticed I was there. He looked down at me as if he was trying to work out who I could be. And then he smiled. It was a sweet smile, but it was full of sadness. Even, I'd say, despair. I'd never seen an expression like it, and I hope I never will again."

Henrik and Maya looked at each other. Neither of them felt too sure about the way this story was going.

Grandmother sighed. "He said – and I've never forgotten his words – he said: "No-one can help me with what I have to do. No-one can help me with what I have to be. But I thank you for trying."

"And then, he asked why I was there, and I told him about Erik. And we stood together and looked out to sea. We talked a little, and then suddenly he cried out, "There's a light! Out there – do you see?"

"And he was right, there was a light, and as the boat came nearer, I saw that it was Erik's. He was safe! I was so happy, I hugged the stranger and danced him round, and when I let him go, he smiled that sweet smile again and said, "I had better go. Your Erik might be jealous." He turned to go, but then he came back again and slipped a ring off his finger. "Here," he said. "Take this. Perhaps it will help you. And if Erik wants to know where it came from, tell him that Prince Hamlet gave it to you, and that I hope it will bring you more happiness than all the riches of Denmark have given to me." Then he bent and kissed my cheek, and he was gone."

"Prince Hamlet!" whispered Henrik.

The grandmother nodded, touching her cheek gently. "Yes. It was. And it's thanks to his ring that we have this beautiful house, with glass in the windows and rugs on the floor."

She gazed sadly into the fire. "If only I could have helped him, as he helped me. I've never forgotten how unhappy he was."

Maya hugged her grandmother. "Do you think father will be home soon?" she whispered. Grandmother kissed the top of her head.

"Depend upon it," she said.

Heather Redman

Usually, Heather's pieces are very short, and we all marvel at how she manages to get a whole story into just a few words. But sometimes, she writes at greater length. She wrote this account of a very special journey she made a few years ago, when she travelled to Sri Lanka for her grandson's wedding. Ed.

A Journey Across Sri Lanka

I could never have imagined that one day I would travel to Sri Lanka. It happened because my American grandson decided that America wasn't for him, and moved to Sri Lanka, where he fell in love with the lovely Nuluka. He wanted as many relations as possible to attend the wedding, so how could I say no? And so I set off with my son, Robert, his wife, Kim, and my nephew, Colin. The wedding was the day after we arrived, but the story I want to tell begins after that, when we set off to see something of this beautiful country.

Off to Kandy

It was Monday and we were off to Kandy, but first we had to pick up the newly-weds. Arriving in daylight, we saw behind the gate a one-level home. Inside we had to take our shoes off. There was a pleasant sitting room with French doors on two walls and sumptuous sofas to sink into, and a kitchen with no ceiling and plants creeping in under the corrugated roof. Rachel, my daughter, exclaimed how wonderful it was and said it reminded her of her grandmother's kitchen. I couldn't see it, except that the sinks were similar.

Hoping the rush hour was over, we all piled back into the bus, and locking the gate, we were on our way.

Well, if the rush hour was over I would hate to be out in it as buses, lorries, cars, motorbikes and toot-toots vied for a share of the road, all hooting and trying to claim a place in the moving masses. Wing mirrors are not a part of any vehicles in Sri Lanka and the only rule of the road is that people on motor bikes must wear a helmet, no matter how many there are on the bike. On one bike driven by a very attractive young lady there was another young lady carrying a very newborn baby, which didn't have a helmet on.

Today was the day I was going to see the baby elephants, something I'd been looking forward to for a very long time. But the sanctuary was gone; it had been sold, and the new owner had turned the whole area into a zoo with exorbitant entry prices. This information put a cloud over the journey but we bowled along and caught up with an older elephant walking along the road in the middle of a small town. It was a pity the traffic kept us moving but we had to get to Kandy so imagine the delight when the driver took a detour and stopped on a quiet road where a couple of elephants were working. Out we tumbled, camera and small change in hand to get close enough to one of the elephants to give her trunk a rub. After we had taken enough photos, we gave a tip to the men working them and scrambled back in the bus to continue our trip to Kandy.

We arrived at Kandy in the late afternoon. The traffic seemed to go faster than ever, with buses chasing each other up and down the roads trying to get to the next stop and get the passengers on their bus – at least six at a time would be racing. Eventually we arrived unscathed at the bottom of a mountain where a sign said 'Hilltop Hotel', and so began the climb up a very steep track that twisted and turned all the way up till we reached the hotel.

Wow! What a hotel! Once inside, we had to walk quite a long way till we got to the main reception room, where we were given a welcome drink of fruit juice. Then we were dispatched downstairs to our rooms. Mine had twin beds, and a drinks fridge which I didn't touch, but a tea and coffee tray which I used often – and the beautiful bathroom with hot water was bliss, especially after the first hotel we'd stayed in, which was very basic with only cold water and no glass in the window.

These windows had stickers on them warning you not to open them in case the monkeys came in, but when you looked past those, there was a panoramic view across the city to the mountains practically all around. Looking straight down you could see the railway station and the bus station, so far away they looked like toys.

After a good night's sleep, we had a wonderful breakfast – bowls of fruit, toast your own bread, pancakes, full English or curry, and waiters floating around filling up your coffee cup at the drop of a hat. Then we went back to our rooms to prepare for our day out in the botanical gardens.

The Botanical Gardens and the Addams Family Hotel

It was a hard day for walking in the heat, but the bit I saw was beautiful. We saw some men digging holes along the path, quite deep holes I thought to put trees in, but no; they were filled with water to filter through the ground to water the roots that were already there, something we're not likely to see in England. Colin and I gave up at that point and went to sit under the oldest tree in the world! While we were there, a gardener came to talk to us about the gardens and his work. Suddenly we saw children filing through the gates all dressed in white. So many came through we thought all the children in Sri Lanka were there. They disappeared deeper into the gardens but a reasonable time later they reappeared from a different place and filed out – we never did find out what they were doing.

Colin and I then moved towards the meeting point where we found a little café and treated ourselves to a very English ice-cream. At the entrance we descended on the gift shop where we bought our souvenirs while waiting for our bus to arrive. Due to the traffic and 'Sri Lanka time', we were waiting quite a while, and were bombarded with men trying to sell us all sorts of things – including a large snake!

Back at the hotel we had a rest. I slept for two hours before Daniel took us off somewhere special for our evening meal. His Uncle Tom had found it on the internet, and had booked the American relations in there for part of their stay.

We left the hotel in pouring rain and slithered down the

mountain, driving across the city and up a hill on the other side, where we were ushered in under umbrellas. An American woman, now dead, had had this peculiar idea for a hotel – it was like something from the Addams family! Inside, it was dark and dismal. The menu was written on a map on the counter in the entrance hall. The room where they took the drinks orders was even darker. Every wall was covered with pictures and at one end of the room, on a coffee table surrounded by sofas, was an enormous thick drawing book, which you were encouraged to draw or write something in, so Kim picked up the packet of crayons and drew the Welsh dragon and flag. The place was scary, and I grew more and more uneasy.

The dining room, which was upstairs, was even worse. I was waiting for a box to open and a hand to appear – it felt as if we were being watched all the time. We were only allowed to order the main course – the rest of the meal was set. The soup was supposed to be coconut, but it was too oily and I couldn't eat it. Next came the main course – two over-cooked fish cakes and a small basin of cold rice on a wooden board. Fortunately I had Robert beside me, so I could pass one of the fishcakes on to him. The sweet arrived in a small coffee cup on a saucer. It was a tiny amount of melted chocolate with a small spoonful of ice cream on top. There was so little I managed to eat it.

Then it was up to the bathroom, which you got to through a bedroom with a four-poster bed. The bath had several thicknesses of heavy black material round it. Opposite was an unfinished concrete block wall with a wooden barrel in front of it with a small round sink and a cold water tap – no towel.

I suddenly felt I had to get out – and fast. I hurried down the stairs and out of the door as quickly as I could, while the others were given a grand tour of the other rooms. I found the bus and scrambled in. While we waited for the others to appear, the bus driver told me he didn't like the place either. The others all appeared to have enjoyed their evening, but I still shudder when I think about that awful night and the overwhelming feeling I had that something very bad had happened there in the past.

Another wedding, and love at first sight!

Back at our own hotel, we got up to another lovely breakfast. One of the sari-clad ladies took me around the breakfast bar and helped me carry my much-needed feast back to my table. Today we were going back to Athurugiriya, so we reluctantly packed our bags ready to leave – but not before Robert and Kim had a last swim.

And as I sat at the poolside I fell in love!

Today there was to be a wedding. The day before, we had watched the large reception room being turned into a sumptuous wedding room. This was going to be a very posh wedding: there were gold and white covered chairs, a dais, and an elaborate sofa covered in red velvet and surrounded by flowers, ready for the photos. Outside, sitting by the pool with my dark glasses on, I watched the wedding dancers and drummers getting dressed, from their white tights to their finished red and white costumes. Like the saris that the ladies wore, there were a lot of layers.

When the tallest and best-looking drummer came out of the room they were in, I rushed across, and asked if I could take his photo. I melted in his sparkling black eyes as he stood and smiled at me – he was lovely!

Then it was time to go back to my room and pick up my luggage. Handing it to a porter, I managed to take a photo of the three bridesmaids waiting for the wedding to begin. The entrance was full of guests arriving for the wedding, so our bus was held up, and we watched and waited while a white runner was laid in the middle of the floor leading to the wedding room. Then a crowd of young men arrived, all dressed the same, with elaborate headdresses; followed by the dancers and drummers. After a short dance they moved on down the white runner and I got my last smile, as my drummer went by, followed by the groom, the young men, then the groom's family and friends. We turned round, and saw that our bus was waiting for us.

A foot massage, and goodbyes

Waiting for the wedding to move through the hotel made our leaving time later than expected, so, with a five-hour journey ahead of us, we set off at speed on a hell-raising ride. We stopped at a posh tea room for a late lunch. Going inside, we saw tables set with whatever tea you wanted to drink, while scattered around were glass cabinets filled with jewellery so you could browse while you drank. We side-tracked this display and made our way to the lift, where we enjoyed a decent meal – I can't remember what I had to eat. We were soon on our way again, dodging the put-puts and motorbikes till we reached Daniel's house and collected up the luggage we'd left behind, before getting back to our original hotel. Only one more day before we had to leave – a pity the cook couldn't make anything except curry!

On our last day, everyone else went to the pool, but I was having a hot oil foot massage. Steve walked me to the massage parlour, which was in another part of the hotel I didn't know about. We took a path down the side of our rooms where there were a couple of houses I presumed were staff quarters. We turned left, then right, and walked between a lake with fish in it and ducks and swans swimming merrily. At the end of a paddy field we turned left and walked past some beautiful houses and bungalows which were also part of the hotel. As the houses came to an end we finally came to the massage parlour – a huge building sectioned off into small rooms.

I took my shoes off at the door and the male masseur

helped me onto a very high bed, telling me to roll my trousers up. This was difficult in the position I was in, but when the doctor came in with a bowl of hot oil and some towels, she said I was fine, and set to work. I shut my eyes and enjoyed the experience – until she mentioned my bad foot. When I told her the pain goes up to my knee sometimes, she told me to roll my trousers higher, and my foot massage turned into a leg massage.

It ended too soon, but when she'd dried my legs and feet with warm towels, the man came back in to help me down and took me into the office. He gave me the most delicious cup of herb tea, then produced a camera and took a photo of the doctor first, then one of me, then a sideway photo of both of us. It seems they were going to advertise this facility and make a brochure to leave in all the rooms – a good idea as we wouldn't have known about it if the menfolk in our party hadn't had a heart-to-heart with the manager. There was also a squash court there, but I wasn't interested in that!

From then on I was walking on air, pain-free and ready for anything – well, almost anything. I lay on my bed until we went for an early supper; before long we were in for hours and hours of travelling and waiting about. For supper I had an egg and tomato sandwich for want of anything better. What a surprise – it was a proper sandwich; at last the cook was learning what I liked! Just as we were thinking of getting an early night, Nuluka turned up with her family to say goodbye and bring us cake and photos to take back for the people who couldn't come, and a big bag of materials for me. After a lot of laughs, a lot of hugs, and a lot of thank yous and promises to go back again, we managed to get back to our rooms to cram the last of our clothes and gifts into our cases. Would we be able to wake up at three thirty, in the middle of the night?

Homeward Bound

We were up and raring to go. Our waiter from the previous day was ready to carry our bags up all those steps to the entrance, where we waited and waited until the bus arrived, with two drivers. With a very sad goodbye to the wonderful waiter who was our mainstay while we were there, we piled into the bus and were on our way. But it was the wrong way! Four passengers wanted to catch a train to the north of the island at six o'clock, so we needed to drop them off first before we headed for the airport. Robert couldn't make the driver understand, so he phoned Daniel and he woke Nuluka up, and she phoned the driver. Between the three of them, we managed to get onto the right road, hurtled through the rain at top speed and drew into the station to find the train still waiting. We said goodbye to the travellers – and lost the spare driver as well. As we left the station, the rain stopped, and we made our way to the airport in daylight. We said a thankful goodbye to the bus driver and were then accosted by porter, who trolleyed our luggage into the airport and then charged us – the cheek of it!

We left Sri Lanka in beautiful sunshine. We had a double seat, which meant I wouldn't have to bother anyone when I needed a walk, but the afterglow of the massage was still with me and I stayed put. The standard of the meals had gone down since I last travelled with Emirates, but we were on our way home so it didn't matter.

We were soon in Dubai and quickly transferred to the right

terminal. Because of my bad leg, Colin and I kept getting moved to the front of the queue. The duty free held no interest for us, so we went straight into the waiting area ready to board – only seven hours to England. Then, horror of horrors, we found there were children sitting in front of us. I expected a journey of screaming, shouting and jumping on seats, but in fact we had a very quiet and peaceful ride. I couldn't believe it. As we were getting off the plane, I congratulated the man in front of me on his two small sons' perfect behaviour.

Back in England at last – but our luggage must have gone on first, because the carousel went round and round with no sign of our luggage till everyone else had taken theirs. Colin was worried about the long drive ahead of him and hurried out of the doors heading for the bus stop, while I trailed behind. Crossing one road was okay – but before I hit the next road, the pavement came up and hit *me*!

I had broken my wrist. So much for all our hopes of getting home soon!

Elephants

They say that elephants never forget
I look into their sad dark eyes and wonder
What they are thinking about
With their wrinkled skin and drunken gait
Their swinging trunks that trumpet now and again.
How we love the elephant!
I remember the childhood rides
On elephants' backs so far up high.
Do they remember the fun we had?
I like to think they do.

Caroline Woolley

It was over 40 years ago that an English teacher friend asked me why wasn't I writing. I'd never thought of it, I said. Well, begin immediately, she said. So I did. I've hardly stopped since and until I joined the world of working sheepdogs, writing was my only hobby.

I believe I can write on a wide range of subjects but poetry is pretty much a 'no go' area – this despite owning a collection of poetry books.

I am now, remarkably, in my seventies and have a family of four with three grandchildren. Unfortunately they all live a great distance from me so that I rarely see them.

On occasion I write to them and they send truly colourful replies.

I live in the countryside, by myself, but among my memories.

To Connemara in North West Ireland – to see the Connemara Donkey

The inspiration for this piece came from a children's book that I received at the age of eight. The beginning section heralded a remarkable travelling holiday – and I found my donkey!

"Can I buy you a drink when we leave port? The only meeting place is the bar," said the rather attractive Irishman. He was walking towards the ferry as a foot passenger, and I was waiting in a queue of cars about to be loaded onto the Rosslare Ferry from Pembroke Dock. Actually I was, at one o'clock on a warm, balmy morning, sitting in a picnic chair parked alongside my car and under a harbour light reading a book. Which is why he had paused to speak to me.

Said Irishman was taken in with my completely 'cool' approach to travel - obviously I was a frequent traveller, he observed in our later conversation. As you might imagine I felt very sophisticated at this unexpected turn of events. After all, having left home a couple of hundred miles since, I was travelling by boat to Ireland to satisfy a childhood fantasy and had not given a thought to possible travel companions.

It was exciting being approached by a real Irishman who was going home to County Mayo to see his mother. He had a very attractive way of speaking and I soon found myself copying his speech patterns – how ill-mannered was that? But he seemed like a nice bloke and I was never likely to see him again – was I?

With an innocent air, he kept buying me glasses of Irish whiskey – lovely. That memory lingers on in a practical sense as I now drink nothing other than Irish in times of medicinal requirement. The time passed far too quickly, conversation had flowed as easily as the whiskey, as had the monumental 'stories' that I told. But before I was found out it was time for me to return to my car for disembarkation.

It was at that point I realized that I had consumed an illegal amount of the Irish nectar and had to drive my car from the boat, past various uniformed officers and take to the open road in a country that I had never visited alone and about which my feeling was somewhat romantic. Fingers and toes were crossed...

The Dorset Snake

She accepted finally, that day at the picnic, that she did not feel included in the family. No one could understand the major difficulties she had with being four years old. Nor did they seem to care that she was frightened all the time, especially since the new baby had arrived.

Her whole shaky world had collapsed when this new human had taken over the mother's time and the father's attention. Such a perfect creature, it seemed. This one did not cry all the time, it gurgled happily and the father was besotted. She could not remember the father being so attracted to her when she was little, but then she had always seemed to be ill, what with the ear abscesses and the tummy upsets. And he was away a lot, something to do with the word "War".

The day had started well enough. It was the father's decision to go to Dorset in the family motorcar and to take the mother's brother, his wife and her cousin Johnny too. Unfortunately the baby had to come along as well, but at least she thought that she might get a bit of time with the father, so long as she was not too sick and did not pick her nose. You always had a problem with the parents if you were travelsick. Oh, and she must not wriggle too much – there was not much room in the tiny car.

It was a warm day, the sort made of summer childhood. As they travelled she wished that the father would not smoke those dreadful white things. She thought they were called Woodbines but this was confusing because the uncle also smoked the white sticks but his were called Players. Very strange! Anyway, the smoke in the car always made her ill, because the father refused to open any windows

"Because of the draught," he said.

He did not seem to realise that the smoke from his cigarette was the cause of her sickness. But then he was not the sort of person who bothered about his effect upon other people. Especially he was not bothered about this serious little girl who was always "there".

She was excited about the picnic. She loved the countryside, the fresh smells and the animals, the naturalness of it all. She had helped the mother prepare the food, carefully spreading the bread with marge and adding either fish paste or jam and remembering not to get the two on the same piece of bread. She was very proud of herself, but no one remarked upon her achievement. The attention of the parents was taken up with the baby being wonderful.

They arrived at their destination after a journey of about 10 cigarettes – the father liked to smoke in series – she was very queasy by this time but had managed not to bring shame upon herself. And she had not touched her nose at all.

While the parents took the picnic things out of the car and were arranging the meal, she took herself away to look for some secret places in the sandy hillocks that were nearby. These hillocks reminded her of the garden of the old house where they had lived before the baby arrived. At the bottom of this remarkable garden were lizards, poppies and butterflies. Just like this place. The grass here was spidery and long and she could not see over the top. Remembering her earlier life, she felt safe. She had not felt so safe for a long time.

The brief moment erupted when she saw, moving towards her, a long windy thing. It moved silently, but definitely, in her direction. What was it? This was something new. She had never seen one of these when she was catching the lizards that parted with their tails or the wasps that she caught to put in her jam jar in the days before the baby.

Safety moved to terror. She screamed. But no one heard her – it was just like her dreams when her screaming went unheard. The thing was getting nearer and nearer and then suddenly the father appeared. And laughed. Oh, the humiliation. He was laughing at her! She had the panic upon her and he laughed!

"It's only a grass snake," he said.

How could he treat her so? After all, couldn't he see that she was only little – aged four? She did not understand about grass snakes and how they are more afraid of you than you of them. How could the father think it was funny?

She only wanted a cuddle, except that as she had never experienced one of those it was difficult for her to define what it was that she needed.

For her the day was ruined, but no one noticed. The father

went back to gurgling with the baby, the cousin to making sandcastles in a bit of earth, and none of the parents spoke to her. She did not remember much of the journey home except that she was sick several times and she took comfort in the recesses of her nose. The parents continued to ignore her and the fathers smoked a lot. Later she crawled into her bed and hid at the far side between the mattress and the wall, deep in misery.

Her nerves became even more taut after that and her dreams developed into nightmares. She could not sleep unless there was a nightlight by her bed and getting up and down stairs was difficult at night because the stairway was dark – she could not reach the light to hide the shadows. She kept seeing snakes everywhere. The mother became fed up with the bother of it all and spent even more time with the perfect baby.

She decided that did not belong with these people called "the parents". She felt she was an intruder in their lives. The baby was acceptable but she was not. Nobody knew or cared about being four years old and frightened.

For many years until she could make choices, she carried on feeling a nuisance, not being listened to, playing second fiddle to the baby and still looking for a cuddle.

And she still cannot go near a snake, be it human or reptile.

Changes

This was the day when I discovered that my childlike aspirations had not gone away, but were merely buried.

It was a hot, cloudless, fierce sort of summer's day when my partner and I came upon a big steam fair somewhere in Dorset. He was reluctant to stay, preferring to return to the multitude of tasks needed to get his next car project started. Far more interesting than the silly old steam fair, he said.

He had to go, that one, not a romantic streak in him!

I was enchanted with all the busyness of my surroundings. Lots of people, lots of steam engines from tiny and middling to very large indeed, lots of noise and bustle. But best of all was the enormous merry-go-round. Very tall, gaudily painted in red and gold and complete with horses with flaring nostrils. And all waiting for me to enjoy. So, I bought an ice-cream in a cone, and clambered aboard.

The partner was so unimpressed and embarrassed with my relapse into childhood that he turned away. Even better, I reasoned, I could enjoy the experience far more without his disapproving stare. In fact he disappeared altogether and I cannot remember how I found my way home that day.

Oh but it was all worth it! Lovely, lovely day. Childhood revisited, remembered, and adulthood balance realigned. And decisions made.

By Hadrian's Wall

I heard frost crackling beneath my feet in the morning air

I heard distant rumbling of thunder – will there be a storm?

I heard stillness

I saw the Blackface sheep that thrive on these hills

I saw the famous sycamore tree filling a gap in the hill

I touched my heart

I touched the roughness of Hadrian's wall behind the tree

I tasted the gentle wind

I smelt the pure morning air and

I wondered how time can be so at rest.

48295315R00092

Printed in Poland
by Amazon Fulfillment
Poland Sp. z o.o., Wrocław